THE LESSON

THE LESSON

Lelisia Hall

The Book Guild Ltd
Sussex, England

The Book Guild Ltd
25 High Street,
Lewes, Sussex

First published 1993
© Lelisia Hall 1993
Typesetting by Book Setters International Limited,
Salisbury, Wiltshire
Printed in Great Britain by
Antony Rowe Ltd.
Chippenham, Wiltshire.

A catalogue record for this book is available from the British Library

ISBN 0 86332 879 2

1

1991. Kathy Herrington, a transfer student, was fresh-faced, eager and excited; this was the first day of her junior year. Her first class, Introduction to Religious Studies, would begin in ten minutes. Judging she had just enough time, she stopped by the Sunshine Diner for orange juice and a doughnut. It felt great to be on her own, she mused, so liberating, and she felt like a mature lady at last. As she walked over to the university she smiled; she could hardly believe she was here. This was the first time Kathy had ever been away from home for an extended period, and persuading her parents to allow her to come so far away had not been easy. Her mother, in particular, had put up a strong fight. But Kathy had won, obviously, having convinced her parents, with the help of her junior college choir director, that the University of Maine had one of the best undergraduate music programmes in the country. Glancing at her watch, Kathy hastened her pace; she certainly did not want to be late on the first day.

Doctor Michael Lenard was reviewing the syllabus for his upcoming class, somewhat dreading having to teach a beginners' course. He had done it so often in the past that he felt he could do it flawlessly with no preparation at all. Realising, fortunately, that such an attitude was detrimental for the students, he would make a special effort to be fresh and enthusiastic. Ordinarily a member of staff would handle introductory courses, but the usual instructor was on maternity leave this semester.

Kathy chose a seat near the front, a practice she had favoured since junior high. It was less distracting. Shyly, but hoping to appear friendly, Kathy glanced around at her classmates. Some seemed as excited and eager to please as she did, while others appeared liable to doze off and slide onto the floor at any moment. The classroom itself was only sparsely decorated; it had a map of the Roman Empire beside the blackboard, a poster of St Augustine on one wall, and a bookshelf along another wall. A series of windows made up the fourth side of the room. What time was it? she wondered. It was nearly 9.05; the professor was late. Kathy was looking forward to meeting this particular teacher, a Dr Lenard, for the school catalogue said he was a graduate of Cambridge University. That fact impressed Kathy immensely, and she hoped he would have a British accent. As she reread his credentials in the catalogue, she pictured a very distinguished, bearded man in her mind.

Lenard, Michael J
Associate Professor of Religion and Philosophy. (1987)
B.A., 1974 Holyrood College, United Kingdom;
M.A., 1977 Cambridge University;
PhD., 1981 Cambridge University, United Kingdom.

By now it was 9.10, and many of the students were becoming restless. Most had hated having to get up so early for this class. *You would think the professor could show up, at least.* Since Lenard had a doctorate, the students were obliged to give him at least fifteen minutes to arrive, but most did so only with annoyance.

'Michael, don't you have a class?' Mark Curry, a member of the English faculty and Michael's close friend, asked as he walked by Michael's office door.

'Yes!' Michael exclaimed and jumped up. Grabbing his textbook, notes and syllabi, he sped off down the hallway.

Mark stood there laughing and shaking his head, being careful not to spill his third cup of departmental coffee of the morning.

Michael rushed down the flight of stairs to the second floor, and then ran down the corridor to room 121. Not a very dignified sight, but he was little concerned about matters like that. Most people knew how Michael was anyway, and they giggled too. Despite his often apparent distractions, he was one of the finest and most beloved members of the entire faculty.

'I apologise!' he said to his annoyed students, some of whom had already started out the door.

As he began calling the roster he looked toward each student as he or she answered. When Michael first saw Kathy he gazed longer than he intended or realised. Something about her reminded him immediately of his dead wife. It was not easy to say what it was about the student that made him think of Angela, although there was a slight resemblance. Kathy was a beautiful young lady anyway, and her male classmates had been eying her too. Like Michael's, Kathy's colouring was dark. Her cheekbones were high, like an Indian's, and she wore little makeup. Michael liked the natural look in women, and compared Kathy's appearance to some of the other young women. Most of them looked phoney, or at best, like they were trying too hard to attract.

It was easier for Kathy to scrutinise Michael without attracting undue attention, and she was slightly disappointed to see that her professor was not a greying, bespectacled Mr Chips type at all. In fact, he did not resemble Kathy's notion of a college professor in the least bit. He was of medium height, about 5'10", she estimated,

7

and probably could have used a few pounds. What truly surprised her was that he was wearing faded blue jeans, a baggy brown sweater and scruffy hiking books. Wasn't there a faculty dress code? she wondered. Furthermore, his shaggy dark brown hair looked like it had not been combed that morning. He did have a British accent, however, and to Kathy's ears, accustomed to the slower drawl common in Georgia, it sounded very elegant. (And she had been thinking she would never be able to understand the Mainers' accents!) Dr Lenard was quite handsome, Kathy thought to herself, if a bit unkempt. Was he married? she wondered, and examined his fingers to see if he wore a wedding band. She did not see one, but knew that did not necessarily indicate he was single. Kathy had always been attracted to men who seemed to need someone to take care of them.

Kathy, being timid and overly self-conscious, could not help noticing Michael's frequent, lingering glances at her. He seemed to catch himself doing it, and would quickly turn his attention elsewhere. What is it? Kathy wondered. Having caught himself staring at the girl again, Michael tried to focus his attention on the various points in the syllabus.

There would be a lot of reading this semester, and essays were to be written every two weeks. Kathy could already tell it was going to require much studying and work, but she felt up to it. Just listening to Dr Lenard speak would make the class a delight for her. For tomorrow he gave them the assignment to write short biographies of themselves. This was one of the ways Michael tried to get better acquainted with all of his pupils. As the class ended, Michael wished he had a reason to talk with Miss Herrington, but he could think of no excuse to detain her. He did not realise, however, the expression that was on his face as their eyes met for the last time that day. It had been a statement of bittersweet longing and great affection. Kathy departed not quite sure what to think, even though she was still not certain she had read him properly. In many ways Kathy Herrington was unusually naive.

Michael thought about Kathy throughout the rest of the day. He was impatient to read her biography the following evening when he got home. As a writer she exhibited promise, but checking her sentence structure and grammar were the least of Michael's concerns right then. Eagerly he read Kathy's paper.

> My name is Katherine Anne Herrington. My mother named me after the author, Katherine Anne Porter, whom she admires. Everyone calls me 'Kathy'. I was born in Atlanta, Georgia on 25 August, 1971, and I grew up there. My father is a lawyer, my mother a housewife, and I have two brothers and a sister. When I was in the fifth grade I started taking clarinet lessons, and I also play the piano and sing. I am majoring in Music, and intend to become a teacher. I chose to come to the University of Maine because of its excellent music programme. My former choir director at the Atlanta Community College was an alumnus of this university, and he recommended that I come here.
>
> My hobbies are horseback-riding, swimming and reading. I especially enjoy science fiction, fantasy, historical romance, and the writings of women authors, especially those from the South. I also enjoy watching movies, going to the theatre, and renting videotapes. Bette Midler, Barbra Streisand, Whitney Houston,

and Michael Bolton are my favorite singers. Meryl Streep and Dustin Hoffman are my favorite movie stars. Right now I live in a residence hall, but I hope to be accepted into the Alpha Chi Omega sorority soon. I don't have a car, but someday I'd like to own a blue Toyota Camry or Honda Civic.

I've not had the opportunity to take any philosophy classes, and the only course in religion I've ever had was called World Religions when I was in the ninth grade, unless Sunday and Bible schools count, but I am sure I shall enjoy this course. I was brought up as a Baptist, but I have always thought learning about other faiths was very important.

Michael was disappointed that Kathy had not written more, but he had not set a length for the autobiographies. What did he expect her to say? he thought. He realised that some students probably felt awkward writing such papers. *So, Kathy was from Atlanta, Georgia.* Michael had never been there, but it made him think of Scarlett O'Hara and Southern belles who talked slowly and wore huge hooped skirts. It also reminded him of racism and "good old boys" with Confederate flags painted on their hot rod cars, and Michael hoped Kathy was not a bigot.

He winced as he calculated that he was nearly nineteen years older than her then chided himself. What kind of outrageous notion was in his mind now? he asked himself. What impossible dream? The girl was not Angela; she just resembled her. Angela was dead; he must accept that cold, heartbreaking fact. She had been dead for nearly six long and lonely years. *Lord, why did it happen? We were married for only a year! Why did You take her, Lord? Surely You could not have needed her more than I did! Are You punishing me?*

He had asked that question at least a hundred times, even though he felt from his religious beliefs that God did not work in quite that way. He did not cause people to die as punishments to others. It was Michael's duty only to accept the will of God, Michael knew, but obediently accepting the deaths of loved ones, especially Angela's and his mother's had been next to impossible for him. He had loved Angela from the moment he met her in 1984, and it had not been only because of her beauty. It had also been her goodness of soul that he had loved, and her gentleness, compassion and love. Every moment they had ever spent together had been a delight, and they had never had any arguments.

Not long before he had met Angela, Michael's mother had died. She had been the only one he felt who had ever truly loved him, until Angela came along. And there was God, of course, but often Michael wondered, despite an intense piety, whether God heard his pleas at all. Sometimes it seemed as if God were ignoring him on purpose, and probably as punishment for all his terrible sins, Michael feared. To almost anyone who knew Michael well, those "terrible" sins were only in Michael's morally oversensitive mind. He was not an angel, of course, but he was very far from being the wicked, defiled creature he considered himself to be. It would depend on whether one was judging with mankind's scales or God's, however, and Michael judged himself by what he was able to know of God's standards. To most ordinary people, those were too exacting and stilted. It was not that Michael was puritanical, because he was not in least bit. He condemned only himself, knowing he lacked the wisdom and the vision necessary for judging other people. He could not see into their hearts, or know their inner feelings and underlying motivations for doing the things they did. It was not his place. For most, if not all, of his life he had been this way.

At eighteen Michael entered Holyrood College in London; a Franciscan seminary which prepared young men for the priesthood. He was ordained in 1977, and was then sent to Cambridge to pursue advanced degrees in philosophy and theology. After earning his certificates from Cambridge, and needing to "find himself" after so much schooling, Michael had gone to a Trappist monastery, Mount Saint Bernard's Abbey in Warwickshire. He remained there for three years. From time to time he was sent into the city on official errands or business, and it was on one of these trips that he had met Angela. (Since Michael was not a professed Trappist, he was almost invariably the one chosen by the Abbot to make these trips to London and elsewhere. Unlike a vowed Trappist, Michael had not been pledged to the rule of enclosure.) He met Angela while touring the British Museum (for the hundredth time), and then ran into her again at St Thomas' Sunday Mass several days later. Michael had never intended to start anything he could not finish, since he was a priest, but he felt instantly drawn to Angela, as she had felt about him. They wrote letters to each other when he returned to the monastery, and whenever he was in London subsequently, they had made arrangements for lunch or another museum tour. It soon became clear to both of them that they were truly in love.

Falling in love was not a problem for Angela. She was single and had always planned to marry some day. It was true that she had never considered falling in love with a monk, but whoever intended such things anyway? Angela was a city girl, born in the London borough of Paddington in 1952, and she was a Roman Catholic of Irish descent. And though she was a free-spirited artist, having been much influenced by the revolutionary verve of the late sixties, it had worried her that she had become romantically involved with a priest.

In time, however, as it became more and more clear how she and Michael felt about each other the taboos did not bother her in the least. It was not as simple for Michael. Deciding to give up the priesthood in order to marry Angela had been the most difficult decision of his life. He never doubted he had made the right one until Angela died. With both parents dead by that time, and because he had no brothers or sisters, Michael had felt extremely alone and lost. Ever since Angela's death, Michael had sensed that God was angry with him, even more than usual. He feared he had failed to notice God's displeasure during the short marriage because he had been so happy, so distracted, he had to admit.

For six months after his wife's passing Michael continued teaching Latin at the parochial school in London where he had got a job after making his decision to marry. But those six months now seemed like dreams; he had few vivid memories of that half year. They had not seemed completely real, and he wondered how he must have managed in the classroom.

It was after he had reasonably recovered from Angela's demise that Michael had come to Maine; he had been too ashamed to return to the Franciscans, and much too contrite to even consider the Trappists again. He made his new start in America using the little bit of money he had been able to save, and the payoffs from Angela's insurance policy. An agency had connected him to the University of Maine, and the job was waiting for him when he got there. It paid more than he had ever earned before, but that fact meant nothing to him. It was a convenience and nothing more.

Ever since that August day in 1987, little over four years ago, when he arrived in Orono, Michael had been living quietly. Though he had made three or four good friends from among the faculty, he had not dated or

13

sought romantic relationships with anyone. He was known as a loner; solitude rarely dissatisfied him. Though he enjoyed seeing a good movie occasionally, and attending the theatre or a concert, he much preferred being at home. He had made extra money from his publications, and in 1989 bought a hundred-year-old hunting cabin that had required a lot of renovation. Having discovered during his years with the Trappists that manual labour relaxed him and helped keep his mind in perspective, Michael looked forward to working on his cabin almost every weekend and during holidays. It was nothing fancy, but he loved being there. He wished he could live there all the time, but it was too lengthy a drive to make daily.

During the school week he stayed in the little apartment he had rented during the first few days after arriving in Orono. At that time it was all he could afford, and, having no vehicle then, the apartment's close proximity to the university had been an added incentive. He still walked to work every day, even in rain or snow, as well as throughout the city, even though he now had a red Ford Ranger pickup truck. Orono was only about seven or eight miles from Bangor too, and the two cities' bus systems were excellent. Unlike most Americans, Michael was not solely dependent on his truck. In fact, he enjoyed walking, and used his pickup only when it was necessary, as when he drove the eighty-odd miles out to his refuge in the deep backwoods.

2

One day about two weeks into the semester, Michael chanced upon Kathy in the Gyro Wrap Restaurant in downtown Orono. It was his favourite place of all to eat, and, as many people shared his appreciation, it was always crowded. It was a hole in the wall, to tell the truth, and cramped. In numerous ways it reminded Michael of the Beatnik hangouts in the fifties and early sixties. Not that he had ever been in a real Beatnik hideaway, but the Gyro Wrap brought to mind the books of Jack Kerouac and the poems of Allen Ginsberg.

At almost any hour Michael might go to the Gyro Wrap, he had learned from experience, he should expect to wait for a table or spot at the bar to become available. That would have been the case for Michael this day too, but he noticed a now familiar dark head seated alone at a table by the streetside windows. Her food had not yet arrived and she was studying.

'May I sit with you?' Michael asked, slightly startling Kathy.

'Yes, of course,' she smiled, and moved her backpack and purse from the table and out of the way.

'You were not waiting for anyone, were you?'

'Oh nah! I'm glad to have someone sit with me. I've fallen in love with Greek food during the last week, but I feel a little bit shy being in here by myself.'

'You appeared to be absorbed in your book.'

'That was just for my nerves, to be completely honest,' she admitted graciously. 'I can't concentrate enough to do any serious reading in here.'

'Do you especially like Hesse, or are you reading *Siddhartha* for a class?' Michael inquired in reference to the book Kathy had pretended to read.

'May I take your order, sir?' a waitress asked, interrupting Kathy as she was about to answer Michael's question.

Michael ordered a suvlaki platter and a large Coke, which were his favourites, and Kathy pondered the waitress's outfit. Kathy believed to her soul the girl, a university student, was wearing a tight-fitting pair of men's black "long John" underwear pants. Michael realised what Kathy was gaping at and grinned.

Kathy turned her attention back to Michael, smiled demurely, and answered his question.

'No, I haven't read any of Hesse's novels until now. I have to read *Siddhartha* for my English class.'

'You must be in Mark Curry's Honour's English.'

'Yeah, how'd you guess?'

'He's one of my closest friends. Hesse is an author whom Mark particularly admires. You're in for a mind-shaking trip in his class.'

'What do you mean?'

Kathy had already concluded that Mr Curry was a dropout from the hippie generation, or that he had experimented with a bit too much acid in those days.

'I mean he's a great teacher, and a wonderful person. He sincerely cares about his subject, and he's able to transmit his enthusiasm, as well as his immense knowledge, to his students.'

'Do you like Hesse's novels, Dr Lenard?' Kathy asked, overwhelmed by Michael's praise of Mark Curry.

'Yes, I do. *Siddhartha* contains much wisdom, as do all of

16

Hesse's novels. I admire that book as well as *Beneath the Wheel*, *Narcissus* and *Goldmund* and *Steppenwolf*. And I would rather you called me "Michael" if you don't mind.'

'Thank you, Michael.' That made her feel grown up.

'Here is your food, ma'am. Your order will be ready in just a few minutes, Dr Lenard,' the waitress said, interrupting their conversation again.

Kathy had ordered a gyro and fries, Michael noted.

'You went to Cambridge University, didn't you?' she asked, knowing full well that he had, but eager to learn more about him.

'Yes, that is right,' he stated matter-of-factly, with not the least conceit.

'That must have been great! Wasn't Cambridge the school used in the movie, *Chariots of Fire*?'

'Many scenes were filmed there.'

'Did you go to the same college as Abrahams?'

'No, he was at Caius College; I was at Trinity, but they're not far from one another.'

'You don't attend classes at Cambridge like we do here, do you? It's really different, isn't it?'

She recalled the move, *Educating Rita*, unaware that it had been made at Trinity College, Dublin, rather than at Cambridge.

'Yes, but one does attend lectures occasionally, or that's the ideal, anyway. You attend as you please.'

'Here's your food,' the waitress said when she returned with Michael's meal. 'Hope you enjoy it.'

'At Cambridge and Oxford, and many other English universities, you're assigned a tutor, and he oversees your course of study. Mostly you choose books to read, or they're suggested, and two or three times a week you meet with your Don, that's what your tutor is called, and discuss what you've been reading. He will give you background information, guidance, and other types of

17

pertinent details. And usually you write an essay each week.'

'Do you have tests?'

'Yes, but not as often as is common here. Usually there is an examination at mid-term, and another at the end of the term.'

'That must make the exams real killers!'

'Yes, they very often are. So, you grew up in Atlanta, Georgia?' Michael despised talking about himself and changed the subject.

'Yes in a suburb called Decatur.'

'Do you miss your home?'

Kathy thought a moment.

'Yeah, a little, but I like it here a lot. It's different though.'

'How is it different?'

'Well, it's already much cooler. In Atlanta right now we'd still be having daytime temperatures in the upper seventies or lower eighties, but we're lucky if we make it to sixty-five here. And people here are nice, but they're not as friendly as people are in the South. I miss by bedroom too. I'm not used to sharing a room with someone else. I also miss my parents, my brothers and sister, and my cat.'

'How old are your brothers and sister?'

'Well, my oldest brother, Jimmy, is twenty-five. He's a lieutenant in the army, and my other brother, Bobby, is twenty-two. He's a senior at Georgia ...'

'The University of Georgia?'

'Yes, and my baby sister is fifteen. She's still in high school. Her name is Lori.'

'What about your cat?'

'He's a grey striped tabby named Jonathan.'

'Do you have your own horse?' Michael asked, surprising Kathy with how well he remembered what she had written in her autobiography.

18

'Yes, I have a red roan mare. Her name is Candy, and I've had her since I was twelve.'

'Where is she stabled?' Michael recalled how when he was a boy he had yearned for a pony.

'At my grandmother's home in Oakwood, Georgia. Oakwood is about fifty miles northeast of Atlanta. I guess you could say it's a suburb of Gainesville; the two communities are rapidly growing together. My grandparents live out in the country, though, and they own about ten acres. I spent most of my summer vacations there when I was little.'

'What were your favourite games when you were a little girl?'

She tried to remember.

'This may sound silly, but I was obsessed with the movies, and I'd watch them on TV and the next day, if I had enjoyed the last night's film, I'd act it out.'

'What films did you especially like?'

'One of the movies that first seriously grabbed my attention was *Carousel*. Maybe it first attracted me to Maine, but it was especially the songs and the story I liked. I have the soundtrack of the movie, and I used to sing along with "When You Walk Alone", "Soliloquy" and "What's the Use of Wondrin" as well as the other songs. Soon after *Carousel* I became aware of *Camelot*. I don't remember how, but I was more familiar with the Richard Burton and Julie Andrews' Broadway soundtrack than with the movie. I didn't even have a chance to see the film until several years after I first started admiring *Camelot*. My best friend and I, and my brother Bobby, used to sing and act them out too. We always had a lot of fun doing "What Do the Simple Folk Do?" '

'What other musicals do you like?'

'*The Sound of Music, Oliver!, Oklahoma* ...'

'Rodgers and Hammerstein much appeal to you then,

19

and Lionel Bart?'

'Yeah, do you like 'em?'

'As a matter of fact I do. *Oliver!* and *Camelot* are indeed among my favourite musicals. Do you like dramatic plays too?'

For the rest of the day songs from the two musicals would be dancing in his head.

'Oh sure! Tennessee Williams is great, and Eugene O'Neill, and Shakespeare, of course.'

'You must have attended an excellent high school.'

'It was all right, but it didn't teach many classes I wanted to take.'

'Such as what?'

'Latin and Greek, for example.'

'Why did you want to learn those languages?'

It was exceedingly rare, Michael thought, for young people of Kathy's age to be interested in the Classics. The young woman was indeed a special one; his estimation of her increased further.

'I guess because I've long felt a true scholar must know them fluently.'

'How did you come to that conclusion?' he asked, studying her closely. She is special, he thought, and enchanting. He loved the way her hair cradled her face.

'From reading and watching old movies. I saw *The Browning Version* with Michael Redgrave on the late show. He played a Greek tutor and I was fascinated. And I read *Goodbye Mr Chips* and lots of biographies. I can't remember everything which convinced me a classical education was the best. Even when you read Edgar Allan Poe you come across Latin and Greek quotations, and in poetry and many other books you find 'em again. I admire Edith Hamilton's books too. In the last century and before all educated persons knew the Classics almost as well as they knew their own language and culture. I really envy you

20

your education, if you want to know the truth.'

'Hey Kathy!' Leisa Palmour, one of the girls who lived in Kathy's dorm said, startling Kathy.

'Leisa, do you know Dr Michael Lenard?'

Leisa scrutinised Michael closely and smiled at him.

'We've seen each other around. You're going out with us tonight, aren't you, Kathy?' Leisa referred to a trip to the mall some of the York Village mates had planned.

'Yeah, sure. I'm looking forward to it.'

'Okay, see you later.' Leisa gave Michael another attentive going over and joined her boyfriend at their table.

'Leisa's an art student,' Kathy explained.

'She has an artistic flair about her. So, are you planning to take Latin and Greek then?'

'I hope so, but I don't think either will be accepted for the Bachelor's degree language requirement for music. I'll continue on in French for that, I guess.'

'You do speak French then?'

'I've taken it for two years already, but I still don't think I'm fluent enough. I can read it far better than speak it.'

'What did you want to be when you grew up?'

'Well, for a while I wanted to be a ballerina. I fell in love with Baryshnikov when I saw *The Turning Point*, and I daydreamed about dancing with him one day.'

'How old were you when you began ballet lessons?'

Suddenly a deafening, bawdy round of laughter exploded from the table where Leisa was sitting with her boyfriend and their friends. It took Michael by surprise, and, composing himself, he smiled shyly at Kathy.

'I was eight,' she answered, and grinned in reference to her rowdy friend.

Leisa was full of life, no doubt about it. Her laugh was a well-known sound in York Village.

21

'How did you decide you wanted to become a music teacher instead?'

'My high school bandleader was a really inspiring person. His wife was the choir director. I loved her as well, and they loved their work as much as they loved each other.'

'Sounds like you had a happy childhood. I always wished I had brothers and sisters, especially during holidays. I always wanted a large family sitting around the dinner table.'

'You don't have any brothers or sisters?' That was something Kathy could hardly imagine.

'No, I was an only child.'

'You're not married, then?' she asked.

Michael shook his head

'What part of England are you from?' In her own way Kathy was as interested in Michael as he was in her.

'I was born in a small town called Lyme Regis. It's in the South West on the coast. It was a wonderful place in which to grow up. I used to love exploring the beaches when I was a boy.'

'England is one of the places I've always dreamed of visiting. I love its traditions and history.'

'Atlanta has a long history too.'

'Atlanta is less than two hundred years old. That's nothing compared to England's heritage. And what kind of history does Atlanta, and the entire South, have? One filled with slavery, and even now, terrible bigotry over a hundred years after the slaves were freed!'

'Well, England doesn't have a guiltless past either, you know. No nation does. It was Colonial Englishmen who brought slaves to America in the first place, and we made a mess of India and Hong Kong.'

They ate in silence for a few minutes, and then Kathy initiated a new line of conversation.

'Do you like music?'

'Certainly. I like Bette Midler and Barbra Streisand too. I especially think the song "From a Distance" is beautiful, but I'm not sure I understand what it means.'

'What do you mean?' Kathy asked, perplexed.

She had never considered what any song meant, at least not seriously. A song's beat was what usually attracted her attention.

'The lyrics say: "from a distance you look like my friend, even though we are at war." Then they say: "God is watching us," and imply He does not see that there are guns and bombs and disease. I believe God is well aware of all our wrongs and sufferings.' Michael grinned sheepishly. 'But I like the song anyway!'

He had suddenly felt he was getting too analytical, which was one of his frequent tendencies. It was the type of mind he had.

'I had never thought about it before, but you do have a point. What other artists do you like?'

Kathy was finding Michael increasingly interesting, but she sensed he was way beyond her in many significant ways.

'Most of those I admire are long before your time. I like the Beatles, for example, and Bob Dylan. And I like Peter, Paul and Mary, and Crosby, Stills, Nash and Young. From more recent years, I admire Jackson Browne, the Eagles and Harry Chapin. I sincerely loved John Lennon too, and it was difficult for me when he was assassinated. I'm a serious lover of classical music too, and my favourite composers are Bach, Palestrina and Vivaldi.'

'To be honest,' Kathy began contritely, 'I don't know as much as I should, as a music major, about classical music. We didn't play much of it in the band, though in the choir we sang parts of *The Messiah*. We danced to Tchaikovsky, Debussy and I don't know who else in ballet. I think their music is very beautiful. I bet I'll be hearing all the classical music I could ever want to hear before long!'

'What music classes do you have this semester?'

'I have piano, clarinet and voice lessons, choir, and Advanced Harmony I. That last class is hard!'

'But you already know how to read music.'

'Yeah, but it's still hard?'

'Who is your teacher?'

Kathy rolled her eyes.

'The holy terror of the music department – Rudy Hoffman! He can be the most sarcastic, arrogant person you could ever imagine. He knows music theory, that's for sure, but he has a serious attitude problem.'

Michael laughed.

'Rudy's not *that* bad, is he?'

'Do you know him?' Kathy was appalled that Michael found her distaste for Hoffman even slightly amusing.

'Yes, but he's not really arrogant. He does come across that way until you get to know him, and he uses scare tactics, I think, to make his students work diligently. He's like a drill sergeant, isn't he? I bet you'll wind up adoring him in the end.'

Kathy stared at Michael as if he had no insight at all into how Hoffman really was, especially in class.

Michael continued smiling and gently laughing.

'You know, Rudy and I occasionally hang out together in the evenings; we play around with guitars, sing a few songs. It would be great if you'd join us.'

Kathy's mouth dropped open, or it might have; she was completely surprised. *Had Dr Lenard just asked her for a date?* She was not sure, but his suggestion was close enough, she felt. She wanted to accept, but wondered if she should. *Getting chummy with teachers was one thing, but Rudy Hoffman was quite another.* She had heard vulgar gossip about him.

24

It was rumoured that Hoffman had affairs with some of his female students. The girls were always interested, however; Hoffman was not as bad, at least, as that Sociology professor who traded good grades for sex.

'When are you and Mr Hoffman getting together again?' she asked, with slight hesitation in her voice.

'Thursday night.'

'Well, I'll let you know before then. Right now I must be going. I've sincerely enjoyed talking with you.'

Michael rose as Kathy did. 'I'm quite finished too. Could I walk with you?'

After paying their bills Michael and Kathy headed back towards the university. As they left the restaurant Leisa yelled a "see ya later" to Kathy; Kathy, slightly embarrassed, gave her a shy wave back.

Orono was a typical college town: bustling, cosmopolitan, and varied. Sidewalk cafes lined the streets; even the Gyro Wrap had some small tables outside. Michael pointed out the Grill; it was another great place to eat, and had the best hamburgers and fried potatoes in town. Like the Greek restaurant, the Grill was always crowded. Michael also indicated where some of the best new and used bookstores were located; he explained that he enjoyed browsing in them during the intervals between his classes. As they passed by a two hundred and fifty-year-old cemetery, Michael confessed that he sometimes brought his lunch out there and ate it among the weather-worn stone sarcophagi. Kathy was not afraid of graveyards, but she did not care to dine in one.

'I must go now,' Kathy said at last.

Michael let her go, but watched her shapely figure admiringly until she disappeared into the Fogler library. What was it about Kathy that he liked so much? he wondered. He felt drawn to her, despite all reason and propriety. Kathy *was* lovely, but he was attracted to her for deeper, more lasting reasons. It made no sense, he admitted; he hardly knew her. Yet he *felt* he knew her extremely well, or he knew her soul.

Michael wanted to protect her as well as guide her in her studies and self-discovery, and he yearned to put his hands through her long, dark hair. It looked soft and silken.

For once in a long while he felt well, like he truly had a purpose to live for. Lately he had often felt he was mindlessly playing along in a meaningless game.

His high spirits persisted until he got home that evening. Then he momentarily regained his socially induced senses of caution and propriety, and worried about what all he might have led Kathy to believe earlier. Recalling the invitation he had given her, he wondered how he might break it without hurting Kathy's feelings. But Rudy would be there too, he rationalised. Maybe it would be all right.

Nevertheless, Michael told himself, he must cool it. Kathy was barely twenty years old! He was old enough to be her father! Furthermore, it was unethical to become romantically involved with one's student, even though it was not as uncommon as many preferred to believe. Rudy had already been given a warning.

But Michael felt so happy when he was with Kathy, and she was much more mature than her years. He felt almost as if they had known each other for ever.

Sitting back, relaxed, in his living room chair, he tried to read more in St Augustine's *On Freedom of the Will*, but time and time again his attention was called away by musings about Angela and Kathy. The two were inextricably linked. Finally giving up on Augustine that night, Michael got ready for bed; afterward he meditated using St Ignatius' *Spiritual Exercises*, as was his wont. He slept fitfully and dreamt that he was going into his mother's bedroom during the last week of her life. The room was darkened and smelled of medicine and disinfectant. She was lying down, her breathing was laboured and raspy; a chair was beside the bed as if a nurse had just gone out for a minute. Michael approached his mother, called to her, and embraced her. It was then that he woke up, tears in his eyes, trembling inside.

When he slept again he had more pleasant dreams. Again he was a boy of twelve spending every summer's day wandering the beaches and hillsides near his house searching for dinosaur bones. Upon returning home he smelled the delicious aromas of his mother's fresh baked bread and sweet cherry tarts; from the front room of the cottage his father's pipe smoke drifted, and Michael greeted his dad as the man was repairing his fishing nets.

Many years later Michael felt an almost otherworldly joy at finally being ordained a priest, and he remembered how nervous he had been as he said his first Mass; his mother had been so very proud of him. Next he was studying Angela as she placed and moulded clay on a sculpture she was doing, and the Beatles' *Abbey Road* played in the background.

3

Having decided to accept Michael's invitation to the jam session with Mr Hoffman, Kathy had obtained directions to Michael's apartment after class ended on Thursday morning. Michael was elated; he had already forgotten the reservations he had entertained on Monday night.

Kathy arrived at 7.30. Hoffman had not yet made an appearance. Although punctuality was one of Kathy's virtues, she feared she had arrived too early, for Michael, upon opening the door, did not appear to be fully dressed.

'Am I too early?' she asked, noticing that his shirt was neither buttoned nor tucked in.

'No,' Michael said, shaking his head negatively. 'You're just on time. Forgive me, I'm the one who isn't ready. Have a seat. Could I offer you something to drink?'

'Yes, what do you have?'

He seemed to ponder her question before responding. 'I have mineral water, cranapple juice, Coca-cola, wine and beer.'

'I'll take Coke then.'

Kathy had been tempted to ask for beer, in order to seem an adult, but she had never yet developed a taste for it.

When Michael returned with her drink, he brought along a plate of banana nut bread and a knife. 'Please help yourself, and excuse me for a few minutes. If Rudy comes, let him in.'

Michael disappeared into the bedroom, and Kathy took the opportunity to examine his living room, and to consider the music he had playing on the stereo (Palestrina's *Missa Papae Marcelli*). It smelled nice in Michael's house, a feature she had noticed from the moment she stepped inside. Evergreen scented potpourri simmered in a burner on a table. The large collection of books and videotapes were among the first items she noticed. Expectedly, many of the books were philosophical or religious, but he also had an impressive library of classics ranging from Plato, Caesar and Ovid, to Dante, Shakespeare and Blake. More modern authors included Sartre and Camus, Joseph Campbell, Thomas Merton, and Kazantzakis. Books by Saint Augustine and about Jungian psychology, among several volumes, were laying about as if Michael were lately reading them. Scanning the videotapes, she recognised the titles of equally classic movies: *Citizen Kane*, *The Seventh Seal*, *Apocalypse Now*, and a great many more. Set apart from the rest, Michael had his collection of screen adaptions of Shakespeare's plays: *Henry V*, *As You Like It*, *Romeo and Juliet*, *The Taming of the Shrew*, among them, and three different versions of *Hamlet*.

On one wall was tacked a parchment, calligraphied manuscript of the *Pater Noster*, the Lord's Prayer, Kathy was almost certain because of her studies in Latin. Kathy read over the vaguely familiar words. '*Pater noster, qui es in caelis . . .* ,' able to translate some of them, but not at all familiar with others. Underneath a coat rack, upon which hung a cowboy hat, a tweed hat, and two canteens, was a Union Jack, and a framed copy of the first folio of Shakespeare's plays hung nearby. Well, Kathy thought, he was not a bad housekeeper. As she sipped her Coke, she continued surveying the room. A crucifix was on another wall, and on a table beside a chair were laying a set of white rosary beads, a book called *Saint Joseph's Daily Missal*, and another volume called *The Liturgy of the Hours*. Kathy took and examined these, flipping through them. As far as she could determine, they were prayer books. While Kathy was scanning some of the prayers, Rudy rapped on the door. Nervously, Kathy invited him inside.

'Good evening, Miss Herrington. How are you?' Rudy asked in his usual abrupt manner.

'I'm fine,' Kathy said as politely as she could, and observed that Rudy had relaxed his attire since she had seen him in class earlier that day.

At school he was always flawlessly dressed, but now he wore dingy, torn blue Levis.

Michael returned, now wearing a red tee-shirt and old, black denim jeans.

'You got any beer, Michael?' Rudy asked.

'You know I do, and just for you.'

Rudy went into the kitchen and returned with a bottle of Heineken. Michael took up his guitar and started tuning it and Rudy did likewise.

'All right, Miss Kathy, what kinds of songs do you sing?' Rudy asked, sizing her up in ways other than musically. A nice little dish, he mused.

'I can sing along with almost any kind, if I know the words.'

'What songs do you know then?'

'Do you know "Annie's Song" by John Denver?' Michael asked, breaking the tension.

Kathy nodded affirmatively, and Michael and Rudy launched into it. Shy at first, Kathy joined in eventually. Although she had confidence in her vocal abilities, she felt out of place. She thought she would have been more comfortable if Hoffman had not been present. During the song Kathy fancied Michael had gazed at her as if he were singing it especially to her, but she was not sure. She did not want to jump to conclusions.

' "Morning of My Life",' Rudy yelled when the time came to start a new song, though Kathy had not been sure at the time what he was talking about. She had never heard of it, but Michael later explained that it was one of the Bee Gee's early hits. The men's voices blended harmoniously, Kathy considered, and they both played guitar extremely well. Occasionally one would shout the name of a chord, and the other would anticipate the direction in which his friend wanted the music to flow.

'What would you like to sing, Miss Kathy?' Rudy asked after the Bee Gee's song was over.

'How about "The Rose?" she suggested timidly.

'Out of my range, but you and Michael should try it,' Rudy said, and went for another beer.

Kathy wondered if she had made a blunder. Michael seemed enthusiastic about Kathy's choice and they started singing. Because her soprano voice was performing beautifully, Michael stopped assisting her in the course of "The Rose", a fact that made Kathy nervous. When she finished, however, even Rudy was impressed.

Subsequently they launched into a long series of pieces, many of which Kathy had never heard before. Despite the fact that she did not sing very much, she enjoyed herself immensely. Just listening to Michael and Rudy was a pleasant treat. They truly were excellent! Kathy could hardly believe how excellent.

'Rudy used to have his own band when he was in college,' Michael explained when Kathy complimented them on their performance.

'Oh! What was it called?'

' "Phoenix Rising",' Rudy said very flatly, as if he were indifferent to it now.

'Do you want more Coke, Kathy?' Michael asked as he started into the kitchen.

'Yes, please.'

'Who is your voice teacher?' Rudy inquired seriously.

'Kay Conelley.'

Rudy shook his head negatively. 'Switch to Jacob Levy or Lee Thompson.'

'Why? I like Kay.'

'You have a very nice voice. It needs training, of course, and technique, but you already have superb control.'

He did not answer her question, Kathy observed, but could not imagine it was because he had little confidence in Kay Conelley's skill and experience. In his own way, Rudy was trying to help Kathy.

'Excuse me, but could I use your bathroom?' Kathy had needed to urinate for nearly twenty minutes, but was too timid to mention it. Now the urge was so intense she could not wait longer.

'Certainly. It's through the bedroom. The light is just inside the door.'

Kathy silently cursed herself. Why did she need to go to the bathroom everywhere she went? Although the bathroom was not especially interesting, Kathy, a very observant person, was sure to note that Michael used Crest toothpaste, and favoured Aspen and Santa Fe colognes. She always noticed such little details because they gave her insight into the people who fascinated her, and when Kathy was intrigued about anything or anyone, she yearned to know all she could. She vowed to remember those colognes in case she ever wanted to buy a gift for him. Since the bedroom was dusky as she passed through it, Kathy was not able to glimpse all she would have liked. She saw that he had a double bed, however, only a small number of clothes hanging in the open Closet Maid apparatus, and more books piled everywhere.

'What instruments do the two of you play?' Kathy asked, as she re-entered the living room and took her seat.

She was more interested in Michael than in Rudy, but she did not want to be uncivil.

'I play piano and trumpet, besides the guitar,' Michael answered.

'I can play almost any type of brass or woodwind instrument, the piano, organ, and all types of guitars. My major instruments, however, are guitar and French horn.' Rudy responded, matter-of-factly. He was not boasting.

'I love the trumpet.' Kathy said, 'as well as the French horn. I play piano and clarinet, but I've always wished I could play an acoustic guitar.'

Scooting close to Kathy where she sat on the sofa, Rudy said, 'Michael and I could teach you how to play.'

Michael handed his guitar to Kathy, and Rudy, with Michael's frequent suggestions and advice, started showing Kathy a few simple chords. Kathy was embarrassed by so much attention at first, but was soon having such fun that she forgot about it.

'So, where are you from, Mr Hoffman?' Kathy had grown to like him more as the evening had progressed.

'I was born in East Germany, but came here with my parents when I was ten.'

'What do you think of the Berlin Wall coming down?'

'It was a great day.' His response was straightforward, with little emotion.

'Now you could go visit where you were born in East Germany, or what was then East Germany.'

'When I was born it was really just Germany.'

Kathy felt like saying, 'Oh, pardon me,' but repressed the urge.

'I wish we had a piano,' Rudy said. 'Come on, let's sing a couple more; then I must go.'

Kathy returned Michael's guitar.

'What do you want us to sing, Kathy?' Michael inquired, seeking to assure her participation.

33

She thought for a few seconds, 'How about John Denver's "Rocky Mountain High"?'

The trio did one other song, "Take Me Home Country Roads" and Rudy said his good nights. Although Kathy had become fonder of Rudy, she was not sorry to see him depart.

'Would you like something else to drink?' Michael wondered, after Rudy had gone.

'No, thanks, I've had enough.'

'You do have a lovely voice.'

'So do you.'

'How is *Siddhartha*? Are you enjoying it?'

'Yeah, and I've almost finished it.'

'What else is Mark having you read?'

'We're going to study pop lyrics next,' she said incredulously, 'and poetry afterward, and during the last two weeks of the semester, we are reading *A Passage to India*.'

'Pop lyrics? That's good. They're not as strange a study for an English class as they may seem. We have had entire courses devoted exclusively to them. With Mark you'll probably analyse lyrics by the Beatles, Bob Dylan, Simon and Garfunkle, Dan Fogelberg, and various others.'

'His tastes are similar to yours, huh?'

'Yeah, Mark and I have much in common.'

'Even more than you and Mr Hoffman?'

'Actually, Rudy and I are distinctively different. We have similar tastes in music, and in a few authors, but other than that, we're not much alike.'

'What authors do you like? I see such a variety on your bookshelves in here.'

'It's difficult to say who my favourites are. Like you mentioned, I admire many. I've read almost all of Thomas Merton's and Alan Watt's books, and I enjoy C S Lewis too. But I've long been a avid reader of the mystics. I can read the same book four times and still find something new in it.'

'The mystics?' Kathy was completely ignorant of them, or even of what the word meant. It reminded her of the occult and astrological topics.

'Yes, people such as Saint John of the Cross, Meister Eckhart, Saints Teresa of Avila and Augustine, and numerous other saints. They had highly sensitive natures, and awesome piety, and were blessed with intense personal experiences of God. Dante was also probably a mystic.'

'What kinds of experiences of God?'

'Visions, mental voices, the Stigmata, unusual insights about the nature and will of God.'

Kathy judged these to be utterly perculiar beliefs. She had never heard of the authors Michael mentioned, except for Augustine and Dante, and they were little more than names; she was not sufficiently familiar with what they had written.

'Do you believe people really see visions? And what is the Stigmata?' Her voice was still incredulous.

'Stigmata is when someone bleeds in the wrists or palms, around the forehead, at the feet, and else where, like Jesus did during the Crucifixion. And yes, I know such things happen. I have no doubts.'

'How can you be so sure?'

'I've never seen a vision, but I am convinced that the Lord communicates with me; He is always near, and hears every word I say.'

'You're Catholic, right?'

'Yes.' Michael became tense. *What if she did not like Catholics?*

'I noticed your rosary beads, and your prayer books. I don't know much about the Catholic religion, but what I've seen of your church services was very beautiful. They seem – holier, or something, than my church's services. What are the *Liturgy of the hours?*' Kathy indicated the

35

black book on the table beside Michael's chair.

He picked it up and opened it.

'They're seven times each day at which prayers are said. Mostly the prayers are taken from the Psalms, but there are also other Biblical readings and hymns.'

'Seven times a day!'

'Yeah, that's how the Breviary was originally arranged, but it has been simplified during the last twenty-five years.'

'Do you say them every day?'

'No, I don't. I used to say them daily, but now I feel closer to God in less formal types of prayer.'

'Are you deeply religious.'

'Yes, I suppose I am. I always have been. Are you?'

'Well, I believe in God, and I try to do what's right. I believe in the Bible, but I don't know as much about it as I should, I guess. I've read parts of it, but I didn't understand a lot.'

'You said in your autobiography that you attended Sunday and Bible schools. You must have studied the Scriptures then.'

'Yeah, but Brother Lawson and Sister McKay never went to college to learn about the Bible. They were just the people who had been going to our church the longest, or who were the most dedicated, so to speak.'

'If they were dedicated, maybe they understood the Bible. You have to study it, and read it many times to comprehend what it is about. Praying for discernment is essential too.'

'Well, one of the reasons I chose to take Introduction to Religious Studies was because I wanted to learn more about the Bible and about all religions. I know only about Baptists, for the most part. I've never been to a Catholic church before, but I've seen the services in movies. One of my favourite stories of all time is *The Thorn Birds*. I love the music especially.'

Michael flinched at Kathy's revelation. *Art copies life; life copies art, which was it*? The correlation brought his head back to earth.

'What's the matter?' Kathy asked with concern. Michael had been quiet longer than he realised.

'Nothing. I was only thinking that we probably won't be studying the Bible, specifically, as much as you may have hoped, not in the class, I mean. We're just going to, as the syllabus explains, briefly examine the major ideas, divergences, and, especially the similarities, between the different traditions. Incidentally, the music you like in that movie, are selections from Gabrielli's *Regina Coeli*, and Franck's *Mass in A Major*.'

'Well, thank you, I'll try to remember that. You don't have them, do you?'

'No, I've searched for them, but so far, I've not been able to find recordings of them. I'm sure they must exist somewhere.'

'Have you ever been to a Baptist church?'

'Yes.'

'You didn't like it, did you?'

'No, to be honest. Since Communion is the central part of the Catholic Mass, I felt the Baptist service was rather destitute.'

'Oh, we have Communion.'

'Not every day.'

'No. You mean Catholics have it every day?'

'Yeah, every time there's a Mass, and in cities, Masses are held two and three times daily.'

'Wow! I didn't know that. We only have Communion once a month, and not even then sometimes. Why do you have it so often?'

'We believe the Communion, or the Eucharist, as it is also called, is the fundamental reason for holding services.

For us, the Eucharist is a re-enactment of the Last Supper; the priest takes the role of Jesus, and the congregation play the disciples. We believe the bread and wine are actually transformed into the body and blood of Jesus, and in consuming them, we are enveloped more by the Lord's grace.'

'Do they taste differently? And you use real wine?' Kathy's eyes were huge with wonder.

'No, they still look and taste just like unleavened bread and wine, and, yes, we do use real wine – Sant'gria, usually.'

'Is Sant'gria a type of wine?'

'Yes, it's a mild, red Spanish variety. Would you like to try some?'

Kathy boldly agreed. She followed Michael into the kitchen, eager to get a look at it too. It was small and the appliances were out-of-date by thirty years, but everything was clean. On the floor beside the refrigerator were bottles of Poland Spring's and Clearly Canadian mineral waters; on top of the refrigerator sat a box of Mueslix cereal, and on the table was a loaf of wholewheat bread. Michael apparently ate a lost of pasta, Kathy reasoned, judging by the eight emptied jars of Classico spaghetti sauce he was now using as canisters. Various shapes of pasta were now in them, as well as assorted types of dried beans.

'Here is your wine, senorita,' Michael said playfully, handing Kathy a wine glass partially filled with a deep purplish liquid. Diffidently, Kathy sniffed it, and afterward took a tiny sip. She was not sure she liked it, and was thankful Michael had not poured out much.

'Well, what do you think?'

'I don't know. It's okay. It's not too strong; I wouldn't like it if it was.' She braved another swallow, willing to give it a fair opportunity. 'I might possibly be able to develop a taste for it. I've just never had any alcohol before. My mom would not allow it the house.'

'I hope I haven't induced you to break a family taboo.'

'Oh, nah! I don't believe it's wrong to drink wine or beer, but many people just don't know when they've had enough.'

'That's sadly true. I don't like beer or liquor, though I've drunk both on occasion. I've never bought either to bring home, except for Rudy. He's not an alcoholic, but he does enjoy a Heineken or two.'

'Ooh! My head is spinning a little bit.'

'Are you all right? Let's go back in there and sit down.'

Kathy felt odd; she had never felt this way before. It was not unpleasant at all, but new to her. She could barely believe she was in such a situation too. *Here she was, feeling weird, to say the least, at the apartment of a man, her teacher, for heaven's sake, whom she had known for less than three weeks! Was he trying to get her drunk? What time was it anyway?*

'It's 12.30,' Michael answered.

Kathy had not realised she had spoken aloud. 'My God! I've got to go. The dorms are locked at 1.00!'

'Okay, I'll drive you. Which one are you in?'

'I live in York Village.'

'Come on.'

Michael dropped her off at the front door, and waited until she was safely inside before driving away. He hoped no one saw them lest the wrong impression was made. What a wonderful evening! he mused and felt happy. He and Kathy had indeed covered a lot of ground.

4

Kathy had begun composing the first essay due in Michael's class a week earlier. It had been entirely rewritten three times and as she approached Michael's office to hand it in, Kathy actually trembled. Michael was grading tests and snacking on a Granny Smith apple.

'Hello,' Kathy beamed cheerfully. 'I've brought my essay.'

Michael smiled, looking up from his work. 'Thank you. Sit down, if you'd like.' He took her essay and laid it aside.

'I had a wonderful time Thursday night.'

'So did I. Did you have a good weekend?'

Kathy smiled and giggled. 'No, I was too busy working on that.' She indicated her essay. 'Did you?'

'Yes, but it was too short.'

'All weekends and holidays are too short! That's a fact of life.'

'True enough,' Michael agreed.

'What did you do?'

Michael's expression brightened. 'I went to my cabin, which I do almost every weekend.'

'Where's your cabin?' Kathy's eyes looked from Michael to the titles on his bookshelves.

'It's about eighty miles northwest of here in Piscataquis county, near Greenville and the Moosehead lake.'

'Do you hunt?'

'No, I go there to relax and recollect myself. It's quiet

and peaceful and I can think more clearly.'

'Does it have electricity?'

'Yes, but no telephone, no cable TV, and no noisy neighbours or constantly busy highways. In the wintertime it is frequently exceedingly quiet. A few hunters may pass through during deer season, and there are occasional fishermen, but they don't disturb me.'

'Are there wild animals?'

'Oh yeah! Deer, moose, fox, raccoons, even a bear now and then. And there are all kinds of wild birds. I've seen and heard ruffled grouse, woodcocks, pheasants and loons. I love it there. I'm able to completely forget the world.'

'Sounds great! But I'd hate to meet a bear.'

'Well, I really wouldn't want to encounter a bear either.'

'Doesn't it get snowed in during the winter?'

He nodded.

'But the main road is kept clear, and my truck has four-wheel drive.'

'But what if the power lines went down?'

Michael laughed gently. 'I don't know how it is in Georgia, but in Maine we always take that possibility into consideration and plan accordingly. There's a fireplace, and the stove is powered by wood or gas, and I have plenty of hurricane lamps and candles.'

'But what about the refrigerator? Your food would spoil if the power was off for days.'

'Are you such a worrier?' Michael asked, teasing Kathy. 'Use your head. All you would need do is put the food in a place protected from wild animals and cover it with snow. Besides, since I don't eat much meat, I could make do without a refrigerator if I had to do so.'

'So, you're a semi-vegetarian?'

'Yes, I suppose you could say so. I like an occasional

41

steak, but hardly more than once every three or six months. If I couldn't eat meat at all I wouldn't miss it. Chicken is all right, and maybe a ham once in a while.'

'Do you like fish?'

'I love fish! My dad was a fisherman. We had fresh seafood every day when I was growing up, if we wanted it.'

'Is your dad still living?'

'No, he died when I was twenty-four.'

'What about your mother?'

Michael's expression became more introspective than usual. 'My mother died when I was thirty. She had been ill for six or eight years. I'm not sure how long exactly, because she hid her sickness from me, as long as it was possible.'

'What was wrong with her – cancer?'

'No, but almost as bad. She had emphysema and congestive heart failure.'

'Did she smoke?'

'Yes, like a nineteenth century factory! I begged her to stop. Even her doctors pleaded with her, but she refused. Sometimes I think she wanted to die.'

'But why?'

Michael bit off another chunk of his apple, pausing reflectively because he could not think of the answer. 'I don't know. She was unhappy and depressed because she could not do all the things she yearned to do. In her life she had been extremely active, always going everywhere; at home she was never idle. Not only did she run the house efficiently, but she had numerous hobbies – gardening, crocheting and knitting, and ...' he added with a wholesome giggle, 'she was always redecorating our home! Every two weeks we had to rearrange the damned furniture!'

'Sounds like my mom, except maybe she doesn't do it

42

that often! My mom will arrange the furniture so that it seems absolutely perfect to her, and it might stay that way for six years, but she's always running up outrageous bills at Macy's and Rich's trying to find the accent piece or the fabric that will give her ideas the grand effect. She's mad!'

'Enjoy her while you may.'

'Didn't you get along with your mother?' Kathy asked quietly and hesitantly. She was afraid she had blurted out another inappropriate question.

'We got along, *most* of the time. I've always deeply regretted that I was not with her at the moment of her death. She wanted me to be there.'

'But you couldn't know when it was going to happen.' Even though Kathy feared she was inept at expressing consolation, she was successful.

'No, but I should've guessed her time was near. She had been in such a grave condition when I last saw her."

'You shouldn't feel guilty about this.'

Michael believed Kathy's advice was wise, but he did feel guilty. Though he had been living as a monk at the time of his mother's death, his life dedicated to God, he felt he had let her down. And, in so depriving another human being, especially his mother, he felt he had failed God. He had not even met Angela yet.

'I'm sure she understands now why you weren't there. Where were you?'

'I pray she understands.'

Where was he? How could he explain to Kathy where he had been? He was quiet for about three minutes, absentmindedly nibbling on his apple. When he gazed into Kathy's eyes again, he knew it would not be a mistake to disclose the truth. 'I was ...' he began and paused, 'in a monastery. I was a monk.'

'A monk! A real monk!' Kathy exclaimed and ruminated over the implications.

There really were monks in the twentieth century! She recalled learning about those of the Middle Ages who kept knowledge from perishing completely, and of the beautiful designs they had drawn for illuminated manuscripts. The movie, *The Name of the Rose*, popped into her mind too. (With Kathy there were always movie associations with almost anything.) She saw ominous, dark hooded figures ambling meditatively down stone Medieval cloisters, and she tried to imagine Michael in a habit.

'Are you shocked?'

'Yeah, very but I think it's cool. Why'd you leave?'

Oh hell! Michael said to himself, and rested his head against the back of his chair.

'I fell in love with a lady and I wanted to marry her. Her name was Angela, and she died a year after we married. It was then that I left England and came to Maine. I couldn't handle my life there any longer.'

'I'm sorry. I guess you miss Angela very much.'

'Yes.'

'Well, I guess I must go.' Kathy did not want to leave, but she thought Michael might prefer to be alone. She felt bad for having pried as much as she had done.

'Do you have to leave?' Michael asked, to Kathy's delight.

'No, I don't need to go anywhere. I just thought...'

'It's all right.'

'So, do you have aunts, uncles and cousins left, at least?' she continued after a short period of silence.

'Yes, but we were never close. They're all in Britain. I haven't seen any of them in at least ten years.'

'My cousins are almost as close to me as my brothers and sisters. I guess you get lonely often, huh?'

'No, I've never been the type who gets lonely. I often miss people I love, and wish they were here, especially my mother and Angela, but I don't mind being alone. I'm

44

used to it, I guess.'

'Golly!' Kathy began, and Michael winced at her unintentional 'taking of the Lord's name in vain', but said nothing. 'I can't stand to be alone much. I have solitary moods occasionally, like anyone, but they usually pass quickly. Whenever I'm alone I must have the television or the stereo playing. I can't stand the silence.'

'I love silence, but I believe it's an appreciation that must be cultivated. The quietude is one of the principal reasons I love my cabin in the woods. There are fewer distractions, and most of those are from inside my head. I'm my worst distraction. It's really deplorable when I'm trying to pray; I can't concentrate because my mind flits from one asinine or trivial matter to another.'

'What do you think about?' Kathy once more felt the tipsy, euphoric sensation she had felt after trying Sant'gria for the first time. Her mind was so attentive to what Michael was saying that she felt almost as though she were swooning.

'When I pray, I endeavour to concentrate on God naturally. I reflect on all He has done for me, and how poorly I've repaid Him. I can't recompense God, but I fail Him even in what I should be able to do. It is very shameful. And, while I'm reading, and a fascinating idea is aroused in my mind, I start exploring it further, and, I turn it around and upside-down until I've examined it thoroughly. I conceive ideas for writing from such origins. Sometimes I don't even know what exactly I'm thinking about. I just allow my imagination to wander, and usually amazing insights are revealed, concepts I was unaware of before. God communicates with me, I believe. The ultimate goal of contemplation is to lose touch with your ego so completely that you merge with a larger reality.'

'What do you mean it's the ultimate goal?'

'Your purpose is to become enraptured by a reality that

is beyond the one to which you are ordinarily accustomed.'

'Is that what meditation is?'

'Yes.'

'Do you practise yoga?'

'No, not yoga, I tried it once, but couldn't get into it. The methods by which I've been guided are called *The Spiritual Exercises of Saint Ignatius*, but I don't always require any formalised system now.'

'What are the . . . whatever you said?'

'It's a book by Saint Ignatius Loyola. He lived in the sixteenth century and wrote a book of spiritual practices and readings that guide a person in meditation.

Detachment from temporal and material concerns is one of the central labours. It takes a while to have success with detachment, and most people are not completely successful even after they've practised meditation all their lives.'

'Are you detached?'

'No way! I have a long way to go.'

'Do you bend yourself into all those funny positions I've seen half-naked, old men doing in India?'

'No, that's Hatha Yoga, a Hindu method. According to Saint Ignatius, you can practise his exercises in whatever posture that is most comfortable for you.'

'I don't know about any of these things. I feel so dumb!'

'Oh no, don't feel dumb! You're not! You've come to college in order to learn more. You are abundantly more sensible than numerous people your age. Much of what I've mentioned, you have had no reason to know about.'

'If I was a Catholic, I'd probably know more about them, wouldn't I?'

'Maybe, but not necessarily. I'm just strange, if you want to know the truth.'

Michael stood up and slipped on his jacket. 'Would you

like to have a soda?'

'Yeah,' Kathy said, and she and Michael started walking down the hallway toward the vending machines.

'This is really nice,' she cooed, still feeling giddy.

'What is? Going to get a soda?'

'No, I mean the conversation we've been having. I really enjoy talking with you. I've never known anyone before who was so interesting.'

Michael rolled his eyes.

'You don't know me very well yet. You'd better hold off on your decision.'

At the drink machines Michael stood staring at the selections, trying to choose between a Doctor Pepper and a Mountain Dew.

'What do you want?' he asked.

Reaching into her purse, Kathy sought some change.

'A Doctor Pepper.'

'I'll get it.' Michael insisted, and inserted fifty cents into the slot.

'Are you sure?'

'Absolutely.' Michael decided on a Pepper too, and led Kathy back to the office.

Beth Frost, a busy body English lecturer, watched them from her office door, as nosey as usual.

Going for a soda with a student was innocent enough, was it not? Michael thought to himself, annoyed with Beth.

'I hope I did a good job on my paper,' Kathy said and took a sip of her drink.

'I'm sure you did.' Michael again gazed into her eyes so seriously, so tenderly, that Kathy hardly knew how to behave.

'I wrote it on C S Lewis's *Mere Christianity*, as you suggested. It was a great book!'

'Did you derive benefit from it?'

47

'Yes, it started me thinking about concepts I've always heard of, but never really thought about seriously. When you grow up familiar with something, you take it for granted you know it well enough already.'

'That's a useful observation. What did you learn?'

'Well, take the doctrine of original sin. When you read the story in Genesis about Adam and Eve, all you usually remember are the snake and the apple; and how God said don't eat of this particular tree, or "ye shall surely die". You think, this is a child's story! Why did God punish humankind so harshly for picking fruit from a tree. Or you get annoyed that most of the blame falls on Eve, on women. But, as Lewis explained, the real sin was disobedience, and when you realise that, it makes a major difference in your level of appreciation for the Adam and Eve story. You say, hey! That's an ingenious parable!'

Michael smiled, 'What else did you learn?'

'The chapter on forgiveness was especially helpful. It examines Jesus's commandment, "love your neighbour as yourself". I'd never thought about it because it seems so obvious, but realising how you feel about yourself, how you love yourself, is important.'

Michael nodded, 'Anything else?'

'Yes, the entire book was illuminating! What about the difference between time and eternity? That's mind-boggling! They're opposites, in a manner of speaking.'

'Yes,' Michael said reflectively, 'And, maybe Lewis didn't mention this, but it's also important to make a distinction between eternity and forever.'

'What is the distinction?' Kathy had always thought the two were synonymous.

'Eternity had neither a beginning nor will it have an ending. God is eternal; He had no birth and He will certainly never die. When we have died and been reborn, if we have merited salvation, we shall henceforward live forever.'

'Can you imagine what it would be like to see the past, present and future all at once, as God does?' Kathy's mind was filled with wondrous awe; until recently she had never pondered such metaphysical concepts.

'No, it's beyond even my imagination!'

'Like I said, it's mind-boggling!'

'Consider also the thought that the Incarnation was not only an historical fact, but is an ongoing event happening always.' Michael hoped to open up Kathy's mind further.

'What do you mean?'

'All right, we're taught God became man in the first century of our era; that the Incarnation was a unique occurrence in time that will not happen again because once was all that was necessary. Instead think how the Incarnation could rather be happening, has always been happening, every time an individual wakes up and surrenders himself completely to God.'

'Then what was Jesus's purpose?'

'Jesus demonstrated how salvation occurs. He redeemed us in the sense that because of Adam's sin we had inherited a rebellious, selfish nature; with Jesus, however, that old nature had been conquered. He is the new Adam. He showed us how life might have been had Adam not been disobedient. But the Incarnation is always occurring since God is eternal and not subject to time.'

'Hold on, you've lost me!'

'As Joseph Campbell explained, "we must die to our fleshly natures and be reborn to the spiritual." This is achieved by conquering the ego-self through total submission to God's transforming grace. Think of the Self, capitalised, as the Holy Spirit. Now this Self about which I'm speaking is not the ego-self, but is linked with the very soul. The Holy Spirit dwells within those who sincerely love God, who are committed to Him, whatever their religion. And the Holy Spirit is God.'

'Are you claiming we're God?' Kathy was shocked.

'No, not exactly. Saint Paul said, "all of us, gazing on the Lord's glory with unveiled faces, (read 'awakened' for 'unveiled'), are being transformed from glory to glory into his very image by the Lord who is the Spirit". Meister Eckhart tried his best to describe these concepts, and he was condemned as a heretic. They are also taught by the Hindus and the Buddhists.'

'What did Eckhart say? Who was he anyway?'

'He was a Dominican monk of the late thirteenth and early fourteenth centuries,' Michael said as he picked up a volume of Eckhart, turned to a much studied page, and began to read:

'"I have often said there is a power in the soul that touches neither time nor flesh. It flows from the spirit and remains in the spirit and is wholly spiritual. In this power God is always verdant and blossoming in all the joy and the honour he is in Himself ... for it is in this power that the eternal Father ceaselessly brings his eternal Son to birth, and that this power also is bearing the Son of the Father, and bearing itself, that same Son, in the single power of the Father." '

'I don't really understand.'

Kathy's head was whirling more rapidly now. She sensed she was nearly upon a profound realisation, but was unable to move forward far enough to grasp it.

'It's almost inexpressible! I can do no better than Eckhart and the other mystics did in explanation. Just think about it. God is eternal; it is always now to Him. The Incarnation, the birth of God into the world, into the hearts of humankind, is likewise eternal; it is happening now throughout the universe. People worry sometimes how men who lived a thousand years before Jesus are to share in salvation, but when you realise the eternity of the event you see there is no problem.' Michael paused, 'I'm sorry. We needn't have gotten into this right yet.'

'But it is fascinating! I'd like to learn more.'

'I could suggest some books for you to read.'

'Yes, all right.' She intended to go to the library the minute she left visiting Michael.

He wrote down a list that included selections by Alan Watts, Joseph Campbell, and F S Happold's *Mysticism: A Study and Anthology*.

'What are you doing later in the week?' Michael asked as he handed her the paper, forgetting caution yet again. He forgot almost everything else when he was with Kathy.

'I don't know of anything in particular. Just going to classes and back to my room to study.'

'Maybe we could go somewhere or do something. We could watch a movie or go out to eat, if you'd like.'

'Yes, I'd love to. What day?' Her excitement was obvious.

'Thursday. I leave every Friday afternoon and go to my cabin.'

'Okay.'

'We'll plan everything more thoroughly later in the week.'

As Kathy walked away, she knew at last that Michael was especially fond of her. She had sensed it all along, but now she had confirmation. It thrilled her. *A grown man was interested in her!* It was hard to believe. *What did it mean? Was he sincere? He surely seemed like it. Why did he find her worth his attention?* The prospects frightened and exhilarated Kathy. *How old was he anyway? Older than thirty*; she remembered Michael had said he was thirty when his mother died. Hurrying back to her room, Kathy roughly calculated a likely age for Michael judging by the years he graduated from college. If he earned his Bachelor's degree in 1974, he might have been about twenty-two years old,

51

she reasoned. The realisation that Michael must be about thirty-nine made Kathy pause. *Thirty-nine*! That seemed ancient! He did not look so old, she thought. His age bothered her for the rest of the evening, but she kept trying to forget about it. She also pondered the conversation, all that stuff about him having once been a monk, and that appreciation he had for silence, those were bizarre, she thought. And what was that other stuff – that talk bout the Incarnation being an eternal, ongoing event? That was definitely weird! She would look into the books he recommended, if only as a means to understand Michael better.

5

'I was wondering what your plans were for the fall recess. Are you going home?' Michael asked after their class one day in mid October.

'No, I'd no more than get there before I'd have to return. I guess I'll just stick around here. Maybe Donna and I will go see a movie or do some shopping. We love to go to the Mall.'

'In Bangor?'

Kathy nodded, 'What are you planning to do?'

'I thought I might ride out to Penobscot Bay. I would enjoy it more if you were with me.' Michael forced himself to look into Kathy's face. He was afraid she would refuse his invitation.

'To Penobscot Bay! I've heard of that. Is it far?'

'It's about thirty or forty miles away, and the bay is beautiful. We'd only be gone three or four hours. You could take your camera.'

'Yes, I would like to go,' Kathy promptly agreed. All her life she had been eager to visit new places. 'What time do you want to leave?'

'Is 10.00 or 10.30 Saturday morning all right?' Michael asked.

Kathy nodded, and Michael started to leave. Then he turned back, having thought of something.

'Could you meet me downtown somewhere so our leaving together wouldn't be so obvious?'

Kathy smiled, 'Ten thirty will be fine. I'll even get to sleep in! And certainly, I'll meet you at the city library.'

Friday crawled by, it seemed to Kathy. She could not wait until Saturday morning. Friday night she was so excited that she slept little, and she changed her mind about what she had planned to wear three times. Donna, Kathy's roommate, believed her friend was demented. *Why in hell did Kathy want to go anywhere with a professor, in the first place, and secondly, why did Kathy care so much about what she would wear?*

Michael arrived to pick Kathy up at 10.15. His Ranger was warm and comfortable inside. As they rode south on route one, they talked and listened to Bach on the stereo. It was a brisk, but sunny day, and the scenery was glorious. All the pine trees reminded Kathy of North Georgia.

'What are you doing tonight?'

'I'm leaving for the cabin,' Michael said, shifting into fifth gear as they entered onto a long stretch of straight highway.

'Oh.' Kathy's voice betrayed the disappointment she felt. She had been hoping they could spend the evening at Michael's apartment watching one of his films.

Michael noticed Kathy's regret, but to invite her to come with him would not only be improper, but also extremely risky. In all honesty, he would have loved for her to join him, but he also feared Kathy would think badly of him if he made such a suggestion.

'Ah, cheer up!' he coaxed. 'You and Donna could go shopping. I'm sure you could find plenty of fun activities. You have other friends than me.'

'You're my best friend.'

'I appreciate that. Maybe you can visit the cabin some other time, okay? We'll find a way to work it out.'

Kathy brightened again, even though she felt ashamed

at herself for revealing her emotions.

'Does this look like England?' Kathy asked, back to her usual self, in reference to the scenery.

Michael shook his head. 'No, not really. The houses and trees are quite different, and so is the lie of the land. Much of England, or, I should say, the parts with which I'm familiar, are rolling hillsides, and haven't nearly as many trees. We have forests in England, of course, but in most places you see only a copse of trees dotting a gentle slope or flat plain. And, in England, you often see ruins of ancient abbeys, or chalk carvings on mountainous out-crops.'

'Have you been to Stonehenge?'

'Yes, I went there on a school outing once.'

'What do you think it is?'

'I believe it's an ancient calendar.'

'Is Stonehenge near where you lived?'

'It's . . . fifty-odd miles away. Tell me about Atlanta.'

'Atlanta? There's little to tell. It's just a nasty, small city with one of the worst crime rates in the United States, and it likes to think of itself as a great metropolis like New York or Los Angeles.'

'You don't think well of Atlanta, do you?'

'I dislike the South. It's a terrible thing to say, but it really is backward in many ways, just like its reputation. There are many good people, it's true, but the majority have an "I don't care" attitude that disgusts me.'

'I'm afraid you might one day discover that such people are not exclusive to any region.'

'I'm sure you're right about that, but especially in the South such people seem to collect. It's the type of culture. The majority of the people are uneducated and, in some cases, downright ignorant, and most of them seem proud of it. I can imagine them in a parade with signs taped on their backs that say: "Stupid but proud". '

'Kathy!'

'I'm serious, Michael. You've never been there. You can't understand how it is. And there's such prejudice and bigotry too and much of those feelings are due to the general ignorance and mistrust of all that's different. And the hatred against Blacks and Jews, and Catholics too, I must admit, are deeply ingrained in peoples' ways of thinking. I mean, Southerners have felt this way for more than two hundred years, right?'

'How did you escape having the same prejudices?'

'I guess because my father is not from the South. He's a Yankee.'

'Where's he from?'

'He was born and raised in Pennsylvania.'

'And your mother?'

'She's a Southerner, but somehow she never believed all the terrible lies, or, if she ever did, she changed her mind when she learned the truth.'

'She must be a good woman.'

'Yes, she is. She's simple, but she cares about people.'

'That is what counts, but Kathy, prejudice is not absent among Yankees.'

'I know, but in the South, the bigots had their way for a very long time. The old hatreds are dying, but slowly. Michael, I've been wondering ever since we left town, what is that music?'

'It's Bach's *Brandenburg Concerti*. Do you like them?'

'I like some of them more than others. Which one is playing right now?'

'That is ... the moderato from concerto six, I believe.'

'It's strange, but I like it. It's kind of melancholy to me.'

Michael seemed to consider her appraisal a moment,

'Yes, I guess you could say that.'

'So, you play the trumpet?'

'Yes.'

56

'Are you good?' Kathy asked challengingly.

'Yeah, I play well enough.'

'What do you play?'

'Some of my favourite pieces are the "Wachet Auf" from Bach's *Cantata One Hundred Forty*, the adagio from Telemann's *Concerto in D for Trumpet*, and Purcell's *Trumpet Voluntary*.'

'Will you play them for me sometime?'

'Yeah,' Michael snickered, 'sometime.'

'You do have a trumpet, don't you?'

'I have. It's the one my parents bought for me when I was fourteen.'

'Do you play it often?'

'Every once in a while. How are your clarinet lessons going?'

'Please, let's not discuss my clarinet playing. I've almost decided to give it up and concentrate on voice and piano.'

'Is it that bad?'

'Yes, I'm just no good at sight-reading, and every time I have to go to my lesson, I literally get physically ill.'

'Rudy?'

Kathy nodded 'yes', Rudy was her teacher.

'Then you should have the same problem with the piano or voice, if sight-reading is a weak spot. Don't let the nervousness you feel towards Rudy stand in your way. He means well, I assure you.'

'I do better at sight-reading in my piano and voice lessons, for some reason.'

'And you have someone other than Rudy for those?'

'Yes.'

'Well, perhaps you should find another clarinet teacher after all, or get over your apprehension regarding Rudy. You'll have to be in more of his classes eventually, and he is the theory professor. He teaches many of the major courses. He is the head of the brass methods class.'

'I don't need to worry about brass.'

'Yes, you do. I've never known a music teacher who was not at least reasonably competent on one instrument from each of the different categories. You already play the piano and the clarinet; that takes care of two – plucked strings and woodwinds. You shall undoubtedly be required to learn a little about a violin or guitar, at least. And, you'll probably have to take up a brass instrument, and something from the percussion section too.'

Dreading the prospect of so much toil, Kathy changed the subject.

'What town in this?'

'This is Belfast.'

'Are we gonna stop here?'

'No, unless you want to stop.'

'Where're we going?'

'I thought Camden would be the most interesting place from which to see the bay. Camden is a great representative of a New England coastal town. It also has many fascinating shops and unique restaurants.'

'This is a very scenic route!'

Kathy's face mirrored the awed elation she was feeling as she took in the rugged coast and the deep, blue water undulating out beyond it.

'Is that Penobscot Bay?'

Michael nodded, enjoying the wonder on Kathy's face. It thrilled him more to see her happy than to see the sights themselves.

'Why didn't you say so?'

'I felt such a marvel of nature could speak for itself. I believe it did so admirably, as I expected.'

They rode on silently appreciating the views for three more miles.

'Mind if I change the music?' Michael asked.

'Of course not. You play whatever you like best. I don't

mind.'

It was impossible to understand or explain, and it was in the tone and manner of Kathy's voice and facial expression, but Michael felt he loved her when she answered his question.

After this development, he caught himself daydreaming about Kathy constantly and staring wistfully at her. He was feeling completely alive again, after nearly a decade of plodding along as if in mourning, and he wanted to hear music that expressed his enthusiasm. Months ago he had made a cassette copy of many of his favourite rock songs, desiring to have them all on one tape. Kathy was not expecting to hear such sounds as "Ohio", "Our House", "Woodstock" or "The Southern Cross" by Crosby, Stills, Nash and Young, or "White Rabbit" and "Somebody to Love" by Jefferson Airplane.

These were followed by many of the Beatles' rowdier numbers, "For What It's Worth" by Buffalo Springfield, and Mick Jagger's and David Bowie's version of "Dancing In the Streets". It was not necessarily the lyrics of these songs, among the many others also on the tape, which Michael liked, but the lively beat of them gave him exuberance. All of them had special memories for him, some of them admittedly bittersweet, and that was another reason he cherished them.

It was 11.15 when they entered Camden. Kathy was enchanted by its picturesque charm. It was just like the images of Maine port towns she had in her mind. Brightly coloured fishing and touring boats were docked along the numerous piers or moored in the harbour, their white sails and multicoloured flags flapping in the breeze. Gulls flew overhead and cawed their mournful cries. Occasionally, Kathy heard a boat's gruff hoot, and it reminded her of a foghorn. Lobster traps and fishing nets were piled along the piers and on the porches of the white houses.

'Would you like to eat something?' Michael asked, as they got out of the truck. He hadn't eaten breakfast.

'Yes,' Kathy agreed.

She had not eaten either, having slept too late to make it to the dining hall. (It had been 4.30 before she had finally relaxed enough to doze off.)

Michael knew where he was going, and Kathy followed, window-shopping as they proceeded down the street. O'Neils was one of the best restaurants in Camden, and that was where Michael led Kathy. The atmosphere pleased her the moment they entered the door. Michael selected one of the famous enchiladas and a salad, and Kathy ordered a taco salad; Michael insisted upon paying the bill, and they went back outside to tour the shops.

Michael had to go into almost every bookshop in town, and Kathy started teasing him for being a bookworm from then on, even though she loved books as much as he did. At the Maine Sweater and Yarn Shop, Kathy went wild over a cardigan decorated with Indian designs. Like Michael, she loved sweaters. Against Kathy's vehement protests, he bought the cardigan for her. Afterward, they spent an hour and a half admiring, puzzling over and discussing the artworks exhibited in the many galleries. Kathy took pictures of Michael and of all the sights as they roamed through Camden. She got many memorable shots of the boats in the harbour, and of Penobscot Bay. It was one of the happiest days of her life, and she hated the fact that it had to end.

At 4.00, having stayed considerably longer than originally intended, they headed back to Orono. By 5.20 they were at the school, and Michael was saying goodbye. He still had to stop by his apartment before making the long drive to the cabin. Since it would be dark before much longer, Kathy was concerned that Michael had to travel so far, but he assured her it would be fine. Reluctantly, she bid him goodnight, wanting more than words were able to express to go with him. If he could have given her a sweet kiss on the cheek, Kathy would have felt better about his leaving.

Though Michael hated to go without her, he knew he must. He had much thinking to do. He made the briefest stop by his apartment to retrieve a few items, and the bag of groceries he had packed last night, got gas at a BP station, and then, without further delay, started out on the long trip to Moosehead. It was a twisting path to his destination; there were many changes of highway, but the roads were good almost the entire way. Ten miles out of Orono he turned off Interstate Ninety-five onto Route Sixteen. Soon he was entering a sportsman's paradise, and, for reasons which escaped him, he recalled the old warning parents had been giving naughty children for generations: "Tommyknockers, tommyknockers, knocking at the door." He had recently read a Stephen King novel, and that bogeyman poem had figured prominently in it. Forty-five minutes later Michael was passing through Greenville, and it was soon time to leave the main roads behind. The rest of the distance would be covered via logging and forestry access roads. By this time, having done so much driving, Michael's foot hurt from pressing the accelerator all day. It would not be much longer, thankfully, and he would be truly home.

Turning finally onto an unpaved road through dense woods, Michael approached the hermitage, as he sometimes thought of the cabin. Michael was thankful to have arrived; he had enjoyed a wonderful, but tiresome, day. It was now only 7.30, but he felt like it ought to be past midnight. Wearily, Michael walked through the cabin, checking all the rooms, turning on the heat to break the chill, and plugging in the compact refrigerator. He put the drinks he had brought inside, even though the refrigerator would not be very cold until morning. Perhaps a shower would help his aching shoulders, Michael thought.

Afterwards he did feel better, and he sat up until 11.00 reading the book on Jungian psychology he had also brought.

That night his bed had rarely felt better and Michael slept soundly. Although his dreams were occupied by many of the fascinating ideas of Jung, instead of the more pleasant thoughts of Kathy, which he would have preferred, Michael awoke on Sunday morning feeling rested. The cheerful songs of the birds helped too.

6

Revelling in nature's variegated marvels, listening to the bird chatter, Michael sat upon a large rock that projected out from the hillside above the cabin. Though it was a beautiful, bright Sunday morning, it was chilly and moderately windy. If there had not been so many trees, he could have seen a great distance. It was not difficult to forget there was a modern world not too far away. It could just as easily have been one hundred and fifty years ago, Michael mused, and he and Henry David Thoreau were exploring the region with the guidance of a Penobscot Indian. Only in Michael's head was heard the conversation he and Thoreau were sharing. It was not uncommon for Michael to entertain such fantasies. All his life he had heard interior voices, and over the years he had learned to think of them as his companions. The fact that he heard the voices most of the time had once worried him, but as he had grown older, he had concluded that they were among the best friends a man could have.

From a spruce tree a red squirrel was cursing the intrusion of his territory. Michael smiled and saluted the little creature; he apologised for his trespassing, and assured the pretty rodent he would soon be gone. True to his word, Michael got to his feet again and started walking. As he walked, he fingered the rosary beads which were in his jacket pocket. *Ave Marias* and *Pater Nosters* spontaneously circulated through his mind. Though he was not presently inclined toward formal prayer, his heart inaudibly conversed with God. Just walking through the woods, or basking in the warmth of the sunlight, were holier experiences than kneeling inside a church.

Whenever Michael was alone and still, Deity spoke to him; or rather, only then was Michael suitably disposed to hear God, who had been speaking unceasingly even during all the stress and anguish of day-to-day life. Usually while in church Michael was too distracted by other people to be carried out of himself. There had been several occasions, nevertheless, most often during the Eucharistic prayer, as Michael had stared at the Crucifix imagining how painful Jesus's suffering must have been, that Michael had lost all awareness of his surroundings. And once, on Good Friday, Michael had imagined the Jesus figure on the cross above the altar was weeping silent, bloody tears. Michael had been contemplating the pain of the crucifixion again, and the reasons why the divine sacrifice had been necessary. How was it possible that many people did not care in the least?

As Michael slowly toured the woods around the cabin, he marvelled over the multicoloured leaves, and over the deep blue brilliance of an October sky. The fallen leaves snapped under his feet and frequently a breeze would send them swirling through the air. Every so often the whooping call of a woodpecker would echo through the forest, and crows caw-cawed as they alerted their comrades to Michael's presence, taking perches on high branches. The crows, and an army of other unseen and unheard animals, watched Michael's every movement. It was likewise with God, but He was also aware of Michael's most secret thoughts.

Back at the cabin, Michael took a seat in a lawn chair. For half an hour he sat in contemplation. Though he had not thought about anything specifically, he would not feel he had wasted time in idleness later. It was peaceful in this wilderness, and Michael felt remote from the existence he led elsewhere as a university professor.

"*Time is out of joint.*" He was living a lie. Something about his life was inauthentic. These feelings were not yet fully conscious, and acknowledging them was only partially successful.

Is this a cross for me to bear? What exactly is it I'm suffering? I am untrue to my most basic self. I am straddling the proverbial fence. I had my hands to the plough and I looked back. To what?

Oh Abba, why does my situation seem so intolerable to me now? Yeah, yeah, the living the lie routine again, and carrying on as though, like most people, I have a goal towards which I hope these empty, vain pursuits of money or career, "the good life," will lead me! Unlike them, I recognise that what I'm pursuing in job and savings, in the collection of more and more, are without meaning. The time I spend here is more real than all I do in the city. The simple life, lived close to the natural world and its rhythms, is what I most value; I have little need for things. They clutter up one's space needlessly, as Bill Moyers wisely observed.

Why don't I resign from my position and retire to the woods permanently? Michael mused. *Why can't I be as courageous as Thoreau had been when he gave it all up to live at Walden pond?*

'I went to the woods because I wished to live deliberately, to front out the essential facts of life, and see if I could not learn what it had to teach, and not, when I came to die, to discover that I had not lived. I did not wish to live what was not life, living is so dear; nor did I wish to practise resignation, unless it was quite necessary.'

Michael had been deeply impressed by those words from the time he first read them at the age of sixteen. They had influenced his rules of life and his opinions in ways he did not even realise. "*To live deliberately,*" Michael had long ago seriously pondered the notion. *What did it mean to live deliberately?* It meant giving due consideration to everything one did, for one thing, and not carrying on, ox-like, as everyone else. It meant realising that each moment was precious, and each experience had a lesson to teach. Being here now was another factor in deliberate living; it was imperative for one to be conscious of the fact that now was eternity. 'Behold, the Kingdom of Heaven is within you.' '... the Kingdom of the Father is spread out upon the earth, and men do not see it.'

How sad it was that most people did not know this. Most would refuse to believe it were they informed. Instead, they lived mechanically; they too often did as society expected without questioning whether it was right for them. 'At certain moments of lucidity, the mechanical aspects of their gestures, their meaningless pantomime makes silly everything that surrounds them,' Camus had written in *The Myth of Sisyphus*. If the Son of God had been unable to penetrate deeply into the hearts of all, who could accomplish such a monumental task?

'A little consideration of what takes place around us everyday would show that a higher law than that of our will regulates events; that our painful labours are unnecessary and fruitless; that only in our easy, simple, spontaneous action are we strong, and by contenting ourselves with obedience we become divine.'

Michael had first read Emerson, the American essayist and poet, at the age of nineteen. Though he had recognised Emerson's profound realisations, Michael now saw even more wisdom. With his monastic background since then, he saw the connection with Benedictine rules of obedience and stability. If he could transmit these lessons to his students, to Kathy, Michael would not fear his life had been in vain.

He felt alive again, and as he examined his existence of the last several years, he was horrified to see all that had been neglected. He had forgotten the dream. *Oh Lord, help me*! he cried.

Going inside the cabin, Michael put a recording of Gregorian Chants on the stereo. He listened to them whenever he felt tense or ill-at-ease, as he did now. The reason for his discontent was still a mystery; it was yet beyond his threshold of consciousness, but it had something to do with his lifestyle.

'Our dreams are the sequel of our waking knowledge.' Michael had memorised many quotations from Emerson and Thoreau, and he added his own discoveries to their observations. 'And our waking knowledge is the sequel of our dreams. One complements the other,' as Jung taught. 'They are connected in the same degree and relationship as black and white, good and evil, life and death, and male and female.'

What was the significance of this realisation? Michael wondered. *What are You trying to tell me?*

The plainsong made him yearn for the peace-of-mind he had felt at the monastery. At the same time, however, he wept for the sweet companionship and abiding love he had shared with Angela. How could the two be reconciled? Why did the Church imply that one could not be devoted to God and love a woman at the same time? He recalled the pleasant time he had spent yesterday with Kathy in Camden.

Oh Lord, I am so desperately confused!!

The abbey bells chiming on the recording made him smile; Brother Giles, who was now dead, had put his entire weight, body and soul, into his bellringing duties at Mount Saint Bernard's.

'Every man has this call of power to do something unique, and no man has any other call. The pretense that he has another call, a summons by name and personal election and outward signs that mark extraordinary and not in the role of common men, is fanaticism, and betrays

67

obtuseness to perceive that there is one mind in all the individuals, and no respect of persons therein.

'By doing his work he makes the need felt which he can supply, and creates the taste by which he is enjoyed. By doing his own work he unfolds himself,' Emerson had written in his essay: *Spiritual Laws*.

Michael laughed as he recalled the annoyance some of the testier brothers had expressed about the quacking of the abbey's ducks. (Thomas Merton had once mentioned a similar incident had occurred at his Abbey of Gethsemani.) Brother Laurence complained the persistent squabblings of the birds interfered with his contemplation. For Michael, it was only the noises of technological humankind which bothered him; especially the clangour of locomotives, speeding automobiles and inconsiderate neighbours. People had forgotten the beauty of silence; many in this age had probably never known it at all.

Kyrie eleison, Kyrie eleison.
Christe eleison, Christe eleison.
Kyrie eleison, Kyrie eleison.
Christe ex audinos.
Pater de caelis Deus, miserere nobis.

Michael sang along with the litany, and meant its prayers with all his heart.

Lord have mercy.
Christ have mercy.
Lord have mercy.
Christ hear us.
God the Father of Heaven,
Have mercy on us.

Michael passed the rest of Sunday reading. It was the

quiet day of recollection he had hoped it would be, a true Sabbath. Kathy was also in his thoughts, and it would have been nice had she been there. With Kathy on his mind, he took out his trumpet and played scales and other warm up exercises. Sifting through his notebook of sheet music, he found the "Wachet Auf" from Bach's *Cantata One Hundred Forty*. Though he needed to practise, he could still hit the high notes. The music relaxed him, and he remembered the joy he had felt when he first worked the piece out by repeatedly listening to Maurice André's performance of it. Nostalgically, Michael dug out his old André LP and accompanied the masterful French trumpeter.

On Monday Michael chopped some logs from a fallen tree and stacked them neatly on the front porch. It would not be long before the first snowfall of the season. Though he always cherished every moment he spent at his hermitage, he especially treasured the cosy, wholesome feeling he always got from being there during midwinter, when two or more feet of snow covered the lawn; the fireplace would have some logs burning in it and Michael would sit in his chair reading by the fire's glow. All he needed, he thought now, was a faithful sheepdog or maybe a malamute, and perhaps a loving wife sitting in her own chair opposite him. Together they would pass the long winter evenings perfectly content just being in each other's company. Frequently they would each look up from their books and smile affectionately at one another and maybe they would read poetry aloud.

Life was never that good, he feared. His daydreaming was suddenly interrupted by reality. He had seen too many films, he thought. But despite all the adverse conditions of real life, it would still be a blessing to have someone to love, to be loved by someone. Maybe the harshness of human existence would be softened if shared.

Michael had always heard that was true.

What was Kathy doing? Michael wondered fondly recalling the curiosity in her brown eyes. He had to admit that he missed her. She had a few changes to pass through, it was true, but he would like to be with her to help make the maturation process a little easier if he could. *Changes?* he thought. He had surely endured many since he was Kathy's age. (One must understand that Michael's use of the word "changes" meant processes of life, spiritual development, as it was used by some in the late sixties and early seventies. It dealt with the phases one must go through to become an authentic human being; to manifest one's inner self which much of society sought to repress.) *Was it possible for him and Kathy to truly be a couple? Were they soul-mates, or was this one of his delusions?* The differences in their ages was a serious issue, he feared. Their life experiences were too vastly separated. They had been shaped by too many divergent standards of belief and values. Nevertheless, Michael was drawn to Kathy; there had to be a reason. It was no longer only because of her resemblance to Angela. As he had gotten to know Kathy better, he had stopped seeing that likeness. Instead, he saw Kathy for the unique and fascinating individual she was in her own right. Yes, she was young, but she exhibited much promise of becoming a dynamic, intelligent lady. Michael wished to do all he could to nurture Kathy's potential; to help her become all he believed she was capable of becoming. In these respects, Michael was much more than a teacher for Kathy; he was a mentor, though Michael would not have admitted, even to himself, the role in which destiny had cast him.

7

Michael forced himself to go to the Humanities Department Halloween party, and he dressed as an eighteenth century gentleman. He hoped he would not have to stay long. The only reason he went was because it was expected, and he was curious to see what Kathy would wear. For a few minutes he talked with Mark, who came as a pirate, and Beth Frost, the silly, flirty English teacher for whom Michael had little use. (She came as a movie starlet; Michael thought Beth's choice of costume was apt.) Beth was the type of woman who demanded to be treated as an equal with men, yet she would use all the stereotypical behaviour woman had struggled long to overcome in order to entice men to do tasks she found distasteful. She would pout and whine Marilyn Monroe-like to seduce men to do paperwork for her or to buy things she wanted. Though Beth did not carry through on the sexual rewards she pretended to promise, numerous men still fell for her games. Michael found it disgusting. Perhaps Mark did too, but he nevertheless played along with her, right into her petite manicured hands. As soon as Kathy arrived, Michael left Mark to his fate.

Kathy was dressed as a 1920s flapper and it suited her, Michael thought. Together they got punch, and then sat and talked, watching the proceedings. It was fun to see everyone's costume. Rudy came as a fencer, which he was in real life anyway. Michael accused Rudy of cheating and they all laughed. Jacob Levy, however, truly went to no great effort; he came as a ghost with the help only of an old sheet. Some of the other costumes were very imaginative.

During a dance Jacob took the spotlight by staging an impromptu haunting. He jumped around in his sheet and twirled like a dervish; it was absolutely insane, but it definitely perked up an otherwise boring party. It was a side of Dr Levy which few had ever seen before and it was refreshing and surprising. To all appearances, Jacob was usually a quiet, unassuming individual, one who could easily be overlooked if not for his brilliant piano playing. Back in the seventies he would have been labelled a 'nerd', though not by those who knew him well, as Michael did.

Soon after Jacob's performance, Michael confessed to Kathy that he could not stand to remain there longer. He hated parties and always had! They left together, as discretely as possible, and started walking across campus. Beth noticed, of course, and she rushed to share the gossip with her best friend, Joan Milton, Kathy's French tutor.

'I like you as a flapper,' Michael said. 'It makes you seem – wilder or something.'

He was in a strange mood. During the last few days he had spent more time with Mark and had been reminded of younger, more rebellious times. Mark was still a hippie, and being around him often brought Michael back to earth. It was good for Michael. Sometimes he got so involved in his religious studies and devotions that he wearied, even depressed himself. Pleasing God was a most difficult endeavour.

'Wilder?' Kathy said, wondering what he meant.

'Yes.' Michael lapsed into silent confusion again. He was not sure what he had meant. 'I don't know what I'm talking about. I go crazy every now and then.'

He gazed at the sky. Michael and Kathy were on the

front lawn of the university, in the oldest section of the school. The buildings which surrounded this area had been the first constructed. It was Michael's favourite place on campus; he thought it the most beautiful. Ancient trees created a tranquil mall under which the pavement walkways crisscrossed. Cast iron benches were scattered throughout and offered peaceful seclusion. It was dark here, dark enough to see the stars through the trees anyway.

'Do you know what tonight is?' he asked mysteriously.

'It's Halloween, of course.'

'Yes, but what is Halloween?'

Kathy had never thought about it.

'A silly holiday, I guess. But it's fun.'

'It's All Hallows' Eve. Tomorrow is All Saints' Day, a solemn feast honouring all holy men and women. Tonight all the damned are supposed to be free to wreak havoc on the earth. Whether it's because we hope to protect ourselves from the demons through disguises, or because a warped person decided we should dress as ghouls, I do not know. Very few people care anymore. Like you said, Halloween is little more than a lighthearted game now, but it wasn't always. Long ago people were absolutely terrified on this night. I believe Jack-O-Lanterns were thought to ward off evil spirits. "Twas a dark and stormy night . . ." as the old gothic stories often began. Men hurried home from their day's work, and their wives and children were glad for them to get there. They would lock up all the doors, leaving their frightful lanterns outside, and place garlic and candles in the windows. The family would all gather around the fireplace and listen as the father read the Bible aloud; maybe they would pray.'

'Are you making all this up?' Kathy said, hoping to lighten the mood.

'No, I'm not. It's true. Have you read *Dracula*?'

'I've seen the movie.'

'Don't you remember when the carriage had picked up Harker and was taking him to the castle? It was All Hallows' Eve and the other people were fearful for Harker's safety, and not only because of his appointment with the Count. They crossed themselves and offered prayers for him.'

'Michael . . .'

Kathy could not explain it, but he was frightening her. She was not the type who scared easily. The fact that the old cemetery was only across the street did not help.

'Are you trying to frighten me?'

'No! Am I?'

He had not really intended to do so, but he had been especially dramatic in recounting his tale. Mischievously Michael grinned.

'Listen to that sound, that sorrowful sound,' he said gravely, and his posture was rapt.

Kathy heard nothing extraordinary, but she listened attentively anyway.

'It's the sound of grieving, of hopelessness and despair. At times like this the moaning of the wind can be confused with the cries of the forsaken and forgotten dead keeping their eternal vigil. There was a night such as this, a night when a young, beautiful woman, much like you, was pressed to her limits. She could no longer accept what the future held for her. She knew she had to destroy herself before she became something she did not want to be. She had quarrelled with her lover; she tried to send him away, but he would not be put off. When he tried to put his arms around her, to comfort her, to keep her safe, she broke away from him and ran off into the black night.

'A storm was rumbling in. Her white dress contrasted against the darkness; he ran after her as she headed she knew not nor cared where. The rain came and soon they were drenched; the winds buffeted them, blowing her long hair wildly. Low branches tore their clothing and scratched them; her small, delicate feet were bruised and mud-stained. The shouts of the lover were lost in the storm, but he ran after her desperately.

'Near the top of the cliff she stumbled over a large rock; crying hysterically she crawled and limped to the edge of the precipice. Her lover reached her, clutched her, spinning her around to face him. Her eyes were wide with terror as the lover held her tightly, as if for dear life; his lips were pressed against her throat. Soon she went limp and he lessened his hold on her. What had he done? He loved her more than life itself and had not wanted to hurt her for anything. Suddenly, with a last surge of energy, she broke free and hurled herself over the cliff. Her screams echoed as she plunged downward. The lover yearned to join her, but it would have done him no good.'

'Michael . . .'

He came out of a trance it seemed.

'What are you talking about? That's an awful story. Is it true?'

He grinned. 'No, but it just as well might be. Actually, it's a speech Barnabas gave on "Dark Shadows", although I changed it slightly.'

'You memorised it!'

'Yes.'

'Why?'

He laughed, 'I'm a romantic, dreaming fool!'

Kathy was speechless; this had turned into such a bizarre night. Michael was staring at her, and then impulsively he kissed her. He seemed to be getting carried away, like he had wanted to embrace her for a long time already. Kathy did not mind; she enjoyed it in fact, but it was so unexpected.

Just as suddenly, Michael pulled away.

75

'I'm sorry.'

He ran off leaving Kathy confused, shocked and tantalised. *Why did he flee?* she wondered. Never had she been kissed so passionately before, and she would not have been averse to more such provocative experiences. Michael's hands had threatened to run amok too, she had felt, and that too was delightful. Slowly Kathy walked to her room.

Michael ran until he felt he would collapse. His heart was beating so fast he could feel it; he was quivering in fact. Simultaneously, he was elated and angry at himself. 'My God! My God!' he said and fell onto the grass to rest and catch his breath. *How can I face her again? What if someone had seen them?* But he did not really care; in some ways, Michael had never felt better.

As he walked home, he continued to think of what had happened. It seemed especially ironic that tomorrow morning, after his class with Kathy, he had to go to church and assist Father Alex in the 11.00 All Saints' Day Mass. *What kind of example am I?* Michael thought.

Other than Mark and Kathy, Father Alex was the only one who knew of Michael's past. Michael had not even told Rudy or Jacob. He did not want it to set him apart in some peoples' eyes, as it might do; and, most importantly, he did not want to talk about his reasons for leaving the priesthood. Speaking about Angela was still too painful for him.

Though Kathy was unable to attend the following day's Mass (Michael had not asked her to come anyway), she surprised him by appearing at his church the following Sunday. Kathy was dumbfounded to see him assisting the priest at the altar! It was true that she knew little about the Catholic Church, but she had understood that Michael was no longer a priest. Seeing him vested, reading the Gospel, and delivering the homily was unsettling for her.

The Gospel reading was Mark 12:28–34, and its primary message had been 'to love the Lord with all your heart, soul and might,' and 'to love your neighbour as yourself.' Michael felt shame in reading from the Bible to a roomful of people; he felt he had been neglecting the Lord. His homily, however, was written from his heart, and it touched nerves in the congregation. One of Michael's purposes in his sermon was to induce people to seriously ponder what it meant to 'love one's neighbour as oneself,' and he recalled Kathy's paper and their discussion on C S Lewis's *Mere Christianity*. Jesus's commandment did not mean we must love the faults of others, since we do not, if we are honest, love such sins in ourselves; yet we have no right to condemn the bad in others either, but must bear with them, realising that most people are probably striving to improve themselves as much as we are. We know how difficult a struggle it is, and should therefore be understanding and compassionate.

All in all, Kathy was impressed by the Catholic service. Though it was not as elaborate as those she had seen in movies, it was beautiful and thought-provoking. Michael looked very handsome in his vestments, Kathy thought. He had read and spoken eloquently too. Kathy was glad she had decided to attend Michael's church and she planned to come again.

'I thought you said you were no longer a priest,' Kathy remarked after the Mass was over. Michael sat down beside her in the pew.

'I'm not. I'm a deacon.'

'But you gave the sermon.'

'Yes, I occasionally do, but, as you saw, Father Alex celebrated the Eucharist.'

'You helped.'

'But he said the prayers and blessed the bread and wine. Those are a priest's significant privileges. I can still do almost everything else, however.'

'Can you do exorcisms?' Kathy had suddenly thought of the gory movie, and her eyes were full of fascination.

'Yes.'

'Have you ever done one? Did the Devil curse you? What was it like?'

'Ah . . .' Michael said and paused. 'I've never done an exorcism such as you're thinking of, fortunately. I don't know any priests who have.'

'Oh, it was just fiction, huh? In the movie, I mean.'

'Well, the priest in the film really did say the liturgy from the Rite of Exorcism, but it's just not performed much. Maybe it used to be done more often, but now we know from medicine and psychology that many of the symptoms that were associated with possession are signs of sickness instead.'

'What do the two candles beside the table mean?' Kathy wondered as she again looked around the sanctuary.

'The candles' light is a symbol for the Light of God, and they stand by the altar as an honour guard would stand vigil at the coffin of a soldier. They add sanctity and holiness. In the Temple of Israel a lamp burned constantly above the Law of God. Likewise, a light is always kept burning beside the altar.'

'What are those things along the side walls.'

'Come on.'

Michael hopped up and Kathy followed him.

'These are the Stations of the Cross. They are used for meditating upon the events of Jesus's last, horrifying day. The first one shows him being condemned by Pontius Pilate. Think how it is our sins that made the crucifixion necessary. The second one depicts the Lord being given his cross, and we think we have a heavy load to bear. The next panel shows Jesus falling the first time. Following it we see Jesus encountering his mother as he heads on to Golgotha. The fifth one depicts Simon helping Jesus carry the cross. We must be willing to help each other too, even when we may be punished for it, and in so doing, we help ease the Lord's sorrow too.'

'What's this? A woman is showing him a cloth with his picture on it?' Kathy did not recall such an occurrence from her Bible reading.

'Yes, that is Saint Veronica. She's the kind lady who wiped the sweat and blood from his face, and his image was impressed on the veil.'

'Really? I've never heard that before.'

'If you believe it.'

'Do you?'

'Yes.'

'Here Jesus has fallen again.' Kathy indicated the seventh picture.

Michael nodded. 'And in the next one we see Jesus speaking to women spectators. He tells them not to weep for him, but for themselves; and we see the disciples deserting him. We must not do as his friends did – run when the going gets tough.'

'And he fell yet again!' Kathy exclaimed as she examined the ninth station.

'Then they strip off his clothes. Can you imagine how humiliating and embarrassing that must have been? That's exactly why it was done too. It was not enough, apparently, to simply crucify him. Then the nails are driven into his wrists and feet. He dies; his body is removed from the cross and laid in the tomb.'

'How many stations are there?' Kathy asked and turned around to count them.

'Fourteen.'

'How often does a Catholic have to say them?'

'A Catholic is not required to say them at all. They're

meditations, as I mentioned.'

'This is all fascinating!'

'What are you going to do now?'

'I have no plans,' she said.

'Let me take these off.' He referred to his dalmatic and stole.

Kathy followed him into the vestry.

Afterwards they walked to the bus stop and caught a ride to Michael's apartment. There they had a snack and spent the afternoon in conversation.

'Are you always the deacon at St Luke's? I mean, what does the priest do when you don't go to church?'

'Alex can say Mass perfectly well without me. I'm only particularly needed for very important Masses, such as those for Christmas and Holy Week. That is not to imply that every Mass is not important, however.'

'Tell me about Holy Week.'

'It begins on Palm Sunday, the day Jesus was cheered as he rode into Jerusalem on an ass, and ends on Easter Sunday morning.'

'The entire week is holy!'

'It is to us. It's also very busy. There are major Masses on Thursday, Friday and Saturday of Holy Week, in addition to the Easter Sunday celebrations. There are often numerous baptisms too.'

Kathy shook her head in awe. She knew the significance of Easter of course, but it was largely associated in her mind with egg hunts and sunrise services.

'I'm sorry about what happened Thursday night,' Michael said.

It embarrassed him to recall his behaviour on that weird evening.

'I'm not sorry,' Kathy admitted, forcing herself to look him in the eyes; it took much nerve for her to be as honest, but she felt it was time.

Michael was stunned; he sat rigidly in his chair completely lost for words.

'Michael,' Kathy said, and he was unable to respond or face her.

A few more uneasy minutes later she called out his name again. He looked at her finally with pained eyes.

'You don't really mean it, do you?' Kathy asked as she perched on the arm of his chair. She referred to his apology.

For several indecisive moments they gazed into each others' eyes. Bravely Kathy kissed him. Almost against his will Michael responded in kind. For a long time Kathy sat on his lap as they continued kissing.

Finally Michael pushed her away; his erection felt like it might burst, and he knew she must have been aware of it.

'Maybe you should leave,' Michael said sadly.

'Do you truly want me to leave?' She refused to believe him.

'Yes.' He lied, but his conscience told him she should go.

Disappointedly, and maybe a little bit relieved if the truth were known, Kathy started pulling on her coat.

'Michael, are you mad at me?' she asked as she reached the door.

'No.'

'Do you promise?'

'Yes, I promise.'

Michael thought of "Dark Shadows" again, the new version this time. He recalled a scene in which Barnabas and his love, Victoria, were making out. The vampire's urge for blood overcame him, very inconveniently, at that time, and Barnabas had pushed Victoria away, told her to leave, because he had not wanted to risk harming her. *What the hell is my curse?* Michael wondered. At this

81

moment he felt as much frustration and anguish as Barnabas must have felt. *Does Kathy understand why I made her go?* He feared he had made a fool of himself.

8

It had been over two weeks since Kathy had spent any meaningful time with Michael. They had seen each other daily only in class, and had usually conversed briefly afterwards. One day she had chanced upon him dining alone in Estabrooke Hall and had joined him, but other than those few occasions, they had spent little time together. During that lunch Michael had addressed several issues that still disturbed Kathy a fortnight later.

'What are you taking spring semester?' Michael had inquired; registration had been scheduled for the following week.

Kathy had explained she was tentatively planning to sign up for Advanced Harmony II and its laboratory, piano, clarinet, voice, Music History 1, and another course that she had yet to decide upon. She expressed an eagerness to enrol in another of Michael's classes.

'Maybe you shouldn't,' Michael had responded, startling Kathy.

She had been expecting him to be glad.

'But I love attending your class! It's the highlight of my day.'

Michael's expression became serious.

'But our relationship . . .' he had begun, and Kathy had interrupted.

'Michael, you're objective when you grade my papers. You've given me only what my work has deserved. Why should our relationship suddenly make any difference?'

'I don't know, but I think it would be better if you chose something else. You don't need another philosophy class to fulfill the requirements. I'm teaching Existentialism, Medieval Philosophy, and Introduction to Eastern Thought. You wouldn't care for any of those.'

'I would, but anyway, I *must* see you every day.' Her voice had been insistent.

'We can still see each other. We can have lunch or dinner together.'

'That won't be enough!' Kathy had blurted out, immediately regretting it.

'Kathy, listen to me, please. I'm trying to do what's right.'

Kathy had known exactly what Michael had been talking about, but she preferred not to face the problem at that time. Ever since then it had seemed to her Michael had been avoiding her. Every day he claimed to have something to do which prevented them from being together; it was usually a faculty meeting or tutoring session. Kathy was clearly lovesick and she felt all the usual pain. Michael's words had crushed her, yet she was comforted by the tacit understanding she sensed was between them: that, despite propriety, Michael did hold tender feelings for her. Nevertheless, she doubted herself. *Who did she think she was*, she asked herself, *to dream that someone like Michael cared for her? What had she to offer him?* It was Friday again. *How could she pass two days without seeing him? How could she endure another lonely weekend?* He was going to the cabin; that meant there was no incentive for attending St Luke's on Sunday. *Ugh!* she sighed. The weekend, usually a time to be cherished, a respite from the routines of college life, but to Kathy it would seem a hundred years long. She groaned, *what has happened to me? I'm a silly fool!*

Oh Michael! she thought dreamily, and pictured him in her mind – his gentle brown eyes, his infectious smile, his disorderly brown hair, and his trim figure. She still relished his accent too, but had grown so used to it already that she only barely noticed its foreignness.

'Hi Kathy, we're having a dorm party. You'll be there, won't you?'

Donna, Kathy's roommate, asked as she approached where Kathy sat on a bench not far from the philosophy building. It was a position Kathy had especially chosen because of its perfect view of the main entrance. Michael most frequently used that door since it was closest to the stairway that led up to his office.

'Yes, that would be fun!' Kathy tried to sound enthusiastic.

With Michael leaving, she had no better plans. Morosely Kathy finished her school day. At dinner she only picked at her food, and afterward retreated to her room as if to hide. It was not possible for long; the other Village mates were already busy preparing for the little party and they were in high spirits.

Twelve young women, mostly aged between eighteen and twenty, sat around on the sofas and chairs, some on the floor, in the lounge. Diet Cokes and Lite beer were the preferred drinks; popcorn, potato chips and candy were the predominant edibles. If a man had walked in unexpectedly, unless he were merely the janitor, the girls would have been ashamed of their dishevelled, unmade-up appearances. Most wore their favourite thread-bare, patched jeans, or dowdy neon coloured tracksuits, none of which did much to enhance any of them. This was a girls' night, and they wanted to be at their most relaxed. Leisa Palmour, the art student from the Gyro Wrap, sat in a window seat with her drawing pad; she could concentrate and still be a lively, witty part of the friendly gathering.

The television, with Sharon's VCR hooked up to it, played a week's worth of 'General Hospital' and 'Santa Barbara' recordings. Kathy was immediately glad she had come. A night of women's companionship would do her good.

A handsome actor on one of the soaps elicited numerous fits of panting and bawdy cheers from the girls. Kathy played along good-naturedly, pretending to agree the man was a 'real hunk,' but privately she much preferred Michael. During a love-scene everyone's attention was rapt, and Leisa made obscene noises similar to those one often heard in such on-screen depictions. Huge Rhonda Scarsdale returned to her room and shortly came back with six-months' accumulations of *Playgirl*, and *International Male* and *Undergear* catalogues; the latter exclusively featured exquisitely attractive young men modelling sexy underwear. These magazines were passed around with much giggling and mock swooning. They had a laughing marathon when Linda and Donna started closely examining the men modelling the bikinis, trying to estimate how 'well-hung' each guy was.

The evening released much tension and served to arouse more 'illicit' curiosity in Kathy. Michael was as attractive as the actor on television or any of the models in the mail order catalogues, in her opinion. *How could I make Michael love me as much as I love him?* she wondered.

'Have you heard about Dr McCauley?' Rhonda asked, eager to spread the latest gossip.

Dr McCauley was the sociology professor whom Kathy had heard made improper suggestions to some of his prettier female students, especially if their grades were low. Everyone perked up to hear the newest story, and Rhonda told it with punch and verve. The man had made yet another conquest. He had called one of his Introduction to Sociology pupils into his office for a mid-term conference. The poor girl's grades were atrocious, and she had been liable to fail if she did not much improve her test scores and write a superior research paper. The girl had, understandably, been alarmed to have been given such a warning, and, as if to offer comfort, McCauley had gotten close to her and started massaging her back, and, well ... you know the rest. They had arranged to meet in his van after dark.

Rudy Hoffman was again the subject of gossip too. It was said that he was now living with a senior nursing student. They had been having an affair, off and on, for two years. Rumour had it also that during the day they sometimes met in one of the private practice rooms in the music building for a 'quickie'.

Kathy was anxious to learn if the other girls thought Dr Lenard was attractive, but decided against mentioning it. She did not want to risk starting a new tale with herself and Michael as the stars. When Jenny, pretty, sweet, but overweight Jenny, asked whom everyone thought were the best-looking teachers, Kathy was thrilled and wanted to hug the girl. Michael was definitely one of those chosen by the majority, but he was also considered to be too eccentric. Jacob Levy did not even rate as fairly attractive, but he did win in the ultra-weirdest category. Rudy Hoffman, Mark Curry, and others whom Kathy did not know, were among those cited as possessing the greatest charm and charisma. It was the athletic coaches who were selected as best-built or all around most desirable. Kathy was proud Michael had rated best-looking, and she felt he would have earned most intelligent, most sensitive, and most interesting too, but those criteria were not up for vote. Jenny even confessed that she had a colossal crush on Michael. Most of the other girls laughed at her, as kindly as possible, and advised her to forget it. Kathy felt sorry for Jenny, but also special and glad to have a secret.

'I would hop into bed with Dr Lenard at a moment's notice, but I can't imagine doing much else with him. He's such a strange fellow. I love to hear him talk, but I can't understand half of what he says,' wild Sheila admitted without a trace of guilt.

'Yeah, I'd bet he's great in bed!' Sheila's pal, Marci, agreed.

'Rumour has it Rudy Hoffman is the greatest stud on campus!' Sharon added.

'Ya'll are all crazy!' Leisa piped; she was from Tennessee. 'Forget about those old men! What about the boys our age? What about John Frankie?'

Several girls squealed with delight.

'Yeah, right – the *boys* our age!' Karen said. 'It's unsafe to go out with most of them, especially the athletes and business majors.'

Everyone laughed raucously.

'I went out with Bryan Woffard last night and had to fight him off!'

'Sure, sure, I don't see any signs of struggle, do you ladies?' Again they all burst out laughing.

'Was he any good, Karen?' Leisa wondered with an insinuating grin.

It was a fun, relaxing evening. Kathy forgot about missing Michael until later when she was alone in her room. (Donna had slipped out to be with her boyfriend.) Kathy wondered what Michael was doing, and she reviewed all he had told her of himself, the many interesting conversations they had enjoyed, the time they had spent together. The day they went to Camden had been a highlight, and she hoped to have such pleasant companionship again soon. Halloween night had certainly been a special event, especially Michael's kiss; and the day at his apartment had been similarly exciting. Again she felt his arms grasping her, squeezing her body closer to his; she smelled his Santa Fe cologne once more and the texture of his costume. If only he were here with her this minute she would run her hands through his hair and kiss him passionately.

'Damn it!' she cursed aloud. That day at his apartment when she had sat on his lap, she had felt 'it' through his pants. *That was proof that Michael desired her, wasn't it? Had his erection embarrassed him?* she wondered. If they had made love, how would it have unfolded, Kathy tried to imagine. *How would she have found the nerve to undress? Hum! This required much planning. Did Michael have hair on his chest?*

She recalled the first time she had visited his apartment. When Michael answered the door his shirt had been unbuttoned. Though she had not paid close attention, she did not recall any hair. *What kind of birth control would be best?* Kathy thought seriously. *Michael was a Catholic, oh my!* All of these and more were important considerations about which Kathy had not previously thought much. It was a good thing, she realised, that Michael had not permitted anything more to happen so far. His concern and foresight endeared him to her more.

It was obvious Kathy was yet a naive virgin. She would have acted impulsively, with the passions of the moment, and there could have been serious consequences. Spontaneity had its role to play, she understood, but in such a day and age as this, and with one's teacher, when one was only an twenty-year-old college junior, it would pay to be patient. All her life Kathy had been overly protected and sheltered by her parents. Her mother was one of those nervous hen types – afraid when her sons wanted to join the football teams; terrified when any one of her chicks got his or her driver's licence, and particularly worried when they started dating. Kathy's mom had not even permitted any of her children to be home alone until they were at least fifteen years old, not for even half an hour!

89

She was always afraid a maniac would break in and murder them, or that the house would explode. It was a miracle Kathy and her siblings were not all hopelessly neurotic. *Maybe they were,* Kathy paused to consider; *who was she to judge?* She loved her mother, but the well-intentioned woman had a major problem when it came to letting her babes grow up.

Mrs Herrington would definitely not approve of Michael, Kathy knew. In her letters to her mother she had only barely mentioned him. The Camden trip was certainly a secret. Her mother had a knack for reading between the lines, or for inventing conspiracies and emergencies when there were none. She was suspicious and paranoid. Not only would Michael's age be objectionable to Kathy's parents, but his religion was another significant drawback. Fortunately, Kathy had avoided being adversely influenced by long held prejudices against Negroes, Catholics and Jews, as she and Michael had earlier discussed, but she was well aware of her parents' feelings. They were not Klu Klux Klan level bigoted. No, they did not hate or wish evil or misfortune on anyone, but they had been fed misinformation and heresy about those minorities all their lives. In the conversation she had had with Michael, Kathy had down-played the extent of her parents' mistrust and lack of understanding, especially with regard to Catholics. Catholics, they believed, worshipped statues, the Virgin Mary and the Pope, and, additionally, they were all drunkards. Until Michael explained to Kathy that actual wine was used during Mass, Kathy had wondered why many people accused Papists generally of being alcoholics. Catholics were also thought to be hypocrites; they went out and sinned without compunction and then went to church and the priest forgave them. It was an old story that had largely died out in other places; in the conservative South such

90

ignorance lingered. Though Kathys's father was not a Southerner, he had lived in Georgia for thirty years. Kathy's mother, moreover, would not even enter a Catholic church. Since Catholics also did not believe in 'getting saved', they were therefore clearly damned; and, they did not hold revivals or practise the 'laying on of hands', at least not in the way good Baptists or the Holiness Congregations did. It was also important to be aware that it was the *Roman* Catholic Church. Had it not been the Romans who conspired with the Jews to crucify Jesus?

Kathy shook her head in exasperation; some of the people who attended her church back home would vehemently denounce you and deny it if you informed them that Jesus had been Jewish. They understood so little, it was pitiful. Complacently they walked around convinced of their salvation; they believed that they were already guaranteed one way tickets to heaven and front row seats.

After preparing for bed, Kathy read more in *The Last Temptation of Christ*, a novel Michael once said he much admired. He had promised to show her the movie, but they had not yet found the time. *Zorba the Greek*, also written by Nikos Kazantzakis, was another film Michael thought Kathy should see. *When*? she felt like screaming. She was eager to see anything Michael suggested, to do anything, if only to be with him.

There was much in *The Last Temptation of Christ* which she did not understand, and much in Kazantzakis's ideas which conflicted sharply with Kathy's Fundamentalist upbringing. She clearly identified with those who rioted and boycotted the Martin Scorsese film. *What could Michael possibly like in the book, especially with his priestly background*? she wondered. *Definitely they must discuss it — whenever*! Still thinking about the novel, Kathy fell asleep and dreamt of Michael.

On Saturday Kathy went to the mall with Donna and

Leisa. With Michael still predominantly occupying her thoughts, Kathy bought a little gift for him – a plaid Cashmink scarf. She told her friends it was for her father. The three of them ate at Knicker's, a nifty restaurant which offered a wide variety of choices, and they laughed themselves silly, and garnered many reproving glances, when Donna, having gotten something in her eye, only made her discomfort worse when she used her napkin to wipe it; she had previously lain the napkin neatly over the remainder of her food – nachos with melted cheese and jalopeno peppers!

The day was rounded off by Donna's discovery that she had locked her keys in the car; they spent an hour longer, with the help of numerous friendly folk and the Bangor police, getting into the Chevy Lumina. (Donna, always accident-prone, was also notorious for locking herself out; whether from her car or her room, it made little difference.)

The next Friday, after another school week of seeing Michael only during class and briefly afterward, Kathy's mood was more depressed. *Had she misunderstood him from the start?* She did not feel she could possibly endure the weekend again without having had at least one significant interchange with him. After lunch, this late November day, she boldly went to his office. To her immense disappointment he was not in. Heartbroken, Kathy slowly went back outside. Then her face brightened immediately. Michael was heading in her direction along with Mark Curry.

'Hello, what are you up to?' Michael asked with a smile.

Mark greeted her and politely excused himself.

'See you later, buddy,' he said and went into the building. He was a most intuitive soul.

'I just wanted to see you. You've been so busy lately,'

Kathy admitted.

'I'm sorry about that. Come on, let's go inside to the office. It's chilly out here.'

Silently they went into the building and climbed the stairs to the third floor. Michael's office was unlocked, as was usual; he tended to trust people.

'I registered, and I took your advice. I did not sign up for one of your classes. Although, I think I might've enjoyed Existentialism or Introduction to Eastern Thought.'

'What did you take?'

'Exactly what I'd planned, and psychology.'

'So, you have Advanced Harmony II to look forward to. You have your favourite Rudy again.' Michael could not resist teasing her about that.

'Yes, the renowned German theorist! I was overjoyed, to say the least, to have another semester with him.'

'Ah, come on, admit it. You quite like him now,' Michael plunged on.

'Oh, he's all right.'

Kathy was not in the mood for games. It seemed to her Michael had taken their lengthy separation too lightly. Situations were not exactly as they had been before. Could he not see that?

'I guess you're going to the woods this afternoon, huh?'

He nodded affirmatively. 'Yes, in a little while. Mark, Dr Cook and I have planned to have a late lunch together first. I'll leave afterwards.'

'Next Thursday is Thanksgiving. We have four days off, counting Saturday and Sunday, I mean. What are you going to do?'

He shrugged. Despite his attempts at levity, he seemed preoccupied.

'I don't know. Are you going home?'

'For four days!'

'I guess it would hardly be worth the effort and expense.'

Several uncomfortable silent minutes passed. Kathy despised such interludes. She never knew how she should behave.

'You're awfully quiet, Michael. Are you all right?'

'I'm sorry. I've a lot on my mind.'

'Do you want me to leave?'

'No. I was thinking perhaps we could do something together. I don't know what yet, but I'll think about it this weekend.'

Kathy was thrilled. Maybe he really had only been busy during the last two weeks. She remembered the scarf she had bought for him, which she had been too timid to give him. Now she planned to present it as a Thanksgiving gift.

'I've been reading *The Last Temptation of Christ*. When we have more time I'd like to discuss it with you, and I'd enjoy seeing the movie too. You said you had it, didn't you?'

'All right. Do you like the novel?'

Kathy's expression informed Michael that she was not sure what she thought of Kazantzakis's book.

'I don't know,' she said diffidently. 'Kazantzakis, or however it's pronounced, was an excellent writer, but some of his ideas about Jesus were shocking.'

'Okay, we'll get into that, perhaps during the break. I'll dig out the movie. Right now, I'm sorry, but I must go.'

Kathy had noticed how Michael kept glancing out the door from time to time. Mark and James Cook, the chairman of the Philosophy department, had passed by the office alerting Michael that they were ready to go. Kathy was satisfied. She had something to look forward to. This weekend might even be reasonably pleasant. It would also behove her, she realised, to organise her complaints with the novel. The book was mostly a ploy she had hoped to use in starting conversations with Michael; she tried always to have interesting topics for him. Though she truly was reading the story, and it had offended her in certain ways, she had not thought about it as much as she might have led Michael to believe.

9

During the last three months Kathy's mind and views of life had been enlarged and refined. With Michael's and Mark Curry's subtle guidance, she had learned to think and to examine aspects of daily life which she had hitherto glimpsed only superficially or unconsciously, if at all. Kathy was intelligent enough, and aware of her former naiveté and immaturity, to realise how profoundly she was being changed. Unlike many other students, she did not think college was an endless party, promiscuous orgy or drinking contest. It was not the place for high jinks, for the time was too brief and precious. All of her life Kathy had yearned to be well-educated; now she had discovered that education meant more than book learning. It was a process of life, and neither the mind nor the spirit could be slighted without a detrimental imbalance.

Always an avid reader, Kathy undertook a reading programme on her own that rivalled those assigned by Michael and Mark. As a child she had learned much by spending hours perusing through her family's set of encyclopediae. She was also a frequent patron of the Atlanta Public Library and the libraries of her schools. When she met Michael, and even beforehand (having been spurred on by what it meant to have attended Cambridge University), Kathy was awed. As their friendship had grown, she discovered her expectations of him were more than fulfilled. If she had been a man, Michael was how she would have wanted to be. Since she was a woman, he was the man of her fantasies.

Because she admired him, she wanted to please him, to justify his encouragements to her, and his interest. Michael was such an excellent teacher that all of his students did their best to meet his high expectations. He had a gift for bringing out the best in his pupils, of recognising where their unique talents lay, and drawing those out to the students' advantages. All of them could not help noticing Michael's special skills, and they often recalled their days in his classes as turning points in their lives.

In the days prior to the Thanksgiving break, Kathy made a special effort to complete *The Last Temptation of Christ*, and she kept notes about what in the novel offended her, and also what she admired or did not quite comprehend. On Wednesday morning after class Michael told her she could stop by his apartment later if she was still interested in viewing the film adaptation of the novel.

With nervous excitement, Kathy selected her outfit especially carefully. She was hoping that she and Michael would engage in more sexual explorations, and she strived to dress as enticingly as good taste would permit. It was impossible to explain, but every time she was near Michael, especially since Halloween night, she felt an almost undeniable urge to push herself against his body and merge into him. *Did he feel the same way?* she wondered. She sensed he did, but that he needed an open invitation, or her permission. Not having an opportunity to spend private time with him lately had been an insufferable agony. *Hell, they had hardly had a moment for each other even in public*! Tonight Kathy hoped they could make up for lost time. She took along the scarf she had bought for him too.

At 8.00 she arrived at his apartment. He greeted her

97

with hot mugs of cocoa and fresh, buttery popcorn. Michael immediately noticed how beautiful Kathy was, but he decided not to mention it. Nevertheless, Kathy was sure she saw a favourable reaction in his eyes.

'Here, I bought this for you,' she said, handing him a gaily wrapped package.

Michael was sincerely appreciative and pleased with the black, grey and red plaid scarf and tried it on for her. It would go well with his coat and Irish tweed cap. He thanked her profusely. Satisfied that her simple gift had given Michael an honest thrill, Kathy relaxed in the chair completely content and at ease. Michael made himself a comfortable nest on the sofa and they started watching *The Last Temptation of Christ*.

Before long the movie was little more than background diversion, for Kathy and Michael were soon engaged in a serious discussion of the ideas it, but especially the novel, examined.

'In the book, Jesus hears the village breathing in its sleep, "how long, Adonai, how long?" What does that mean?' Kathy asked as she watched Willem Defoe enact a scene in which a young man was having a nightmare.

'*Adonai* is a Hebrew word meaning God or Lord. The village inhabitants, who are a symbol for the entire people of Israel, are asking God when He is going to send the Messiah to redeem them, to free them of foreign domination, and to usher in the age of peace.'

'I don't like how the author portrayed Jesus as a crossmaker. Why did he do that?'

'Irony. Foreshadowing. Jesus tells Judas that he makes crosses so that God will be angry with him.'

'But why would Jesus want God to be angry with him?'

'He is afraid. Visions and dreams have intimated to him that God has a special destiny planned, and it is not only of utmost importance, but is also excruciatingly painful.

98

Put yourself into Jesus's place. How would you feel?'

'But Jesus knew what he had to do when he agreed to become a man. Suffering for the sins of humanity was the whole reason he came into this world.'

'Don't criticise Kazantzakis's viewpoint, but try to understand his themes and purposes. Whether you agree or not isn't the point. Kazantzakis hoped people could better identify with a very human depiction of Jesus. I certainly do.'

'What about this dream?'

Kathy turned to page eighty-one of the novel and read: "He had a dream. The world seemed to be a green meadow, all in bloom, and God an olive-skinned shepherd boy with two twisted horns, newly grown and still tender, who sat next to a cistern of water and played his pipe".

It goes on to describe how as the boy-God played his pipe, animal creation grew out of the soil and grass, and leaves of the trees. Then all the animals started coupling, and God became angry, stopped playing the music, and everything vanished. What does that mean? Jesus woke from this dream ashamed about having such sexual impressions in his head.'

Michael rested his head on the back of the sofa and thought several minutes.

'It reminds me of a Greek or Hindu story. The boy-God with a pipe makes me think of Pan, and the music bringing forth creatures from the earth is connected with myths about the Hindu god Shiva; it could also have something to do with Orpheus, perhaps. As Shiva dances he automatically creates, and as long as he dances, the world will continue. I think it would be illuminating for you to read the *Bhagavad Gita* and the *Upanishads*. They would help you to recognise the numerous Hindu ideas in the novel. Have you ever studied Hinduism?'

'Only in the World Religions class I had in the ninth grade, but that's been such a long time. Mr Curry said a little about it when we discussed *Siddhartha*. We didn't get so involved as to study their scriptures. I've heard of those books you mentioned, but I don't know what they're about. Does the Roman Catholic church encourage its followers to study the holy scriptures of other religions?'

'No, I wouldn't say the Church encourages such studies.'

'Then how can you believe what your church would say was wrong?'

'I listen to an inner voice and I pray for wisdom and discernment. Believe it or not, but there are certain aspects of Catholic doctrine which I cannot buy.'

'Such as what?' Kathy was especially interested in this.

'Maybe I misunderstand, but I think the Church relies too heavily on guilt to enforce its doctrines and codes of behaviour. I have a terrible guilt complex; it's even crippling in some ways. Even though I recognise it, I cannot quite overcome it. Believe me, I've tried!'

'So what's the *Gita* about?'

Kathy would have liked to hear what Michael felt guilty about, but she was too shy to ask; she thought it might be tactless.

'The *Bhagavad Gita* is part of the Hindu epic, the *Mahabarata*. In the *Gita* two regal and related families are about to wage a war against each other. One of the soldiers, Arjuna, has a conversation with the god Krishna, and through this all of Hinduism's most fundamental doctrines are explored. You must read it!' Michael said excitedly, and quickly located one of his copies and handed it to Kathy.

She flipped through it and saw that Michael had underlined his favourite passages, or made marginal notations.

100

'The *Upanishads* would also be beneficial for you. Joseph Campbell made use of many of their stories in his books and lectures. Try not to allow your Baptist upbringing to stop you from investigating the other religious and philosophical traditions with an open mind.'

'I'll try. Okay, I'll read the *Bhagavad Gita* and let you know what I think of it.'

On the screen they watched as Mary Magdalene said hostilely to Jesus, "You're the same as all the others, only you can't admit it," when he came to her brothel to beg her forgiveness. She also accused him of lacking the courage to be a man, which, in Magdalene's opinion, meant having sex with a woman.

'But Jesus wasn't like other men!' Kathy insisted angrily. This was one of the objections she had to Kazantzakis's Jesus. 'Can't she see that?'

She doesn't want to see it. She's hurt because she loves him and he cannot return her love as she thinks he should.'

'Well, why does he feel like he should apologise to her, for heaven's sake?'

'Because he feels responsible for leading her into a life of prostitution. Remember, when the two had been children they had engaged in seemingly harmless touching games, and Jesus feels these introduced Mary to the pleasures of the flesh. Because he was unable to marry her later, he blames himself for Mary's bitter, spiteful anger. Perhaps because his religious devotion prevented Jesus from loving her as a woman, she turned to a lifestyle diametrically opposed to the career Jesus had chosen. And since he's on his way to the desert monastery, he must reconcile himself to all whom he has hurt. That's the Law.'

' "If you bring your gift to the altar and then recall that your brother has anything against you, leave your gift, go first to be reconciled with your brother, and then come

101

and offer your gift." ' Kathy quoted, surprising herself.

'Exactly!' Michael smiled.

'But where did Kazantzakis get the idea that Jesus and Mary Magdalene grew up together and were in love?'

'He made it up, I guess, unless he took it from some of the so-called lost books of the Bible. It doesn't matter. The use he makes of the situation is all that's important.'

For a few minutes they watched the film in silence. Michael was trying to understand Kathy's point of view. It was difficult to realise what seemed so obvious to him might justifiably not be to everyone else.

'The movie is not nearly as clear as the book, is it? I mean it's a good film adaptation, but much had to be omitted,' Michael remarked and Kathy agreed. 'Do you see the dichotomy represented by Jesus and Judas? Though they each have the goal of liberating people, their beliefs and methods for accomplishing this are in contrast to one another. Judas is a man of the flesh, of the world; he's a militaristic revolutionary; self-righteous and na-tionalistic. To him it is this world that is of greatest importance. Jesus is a man of the spirit, of heaven; he's a prophet of love and peace; when Judas speaks of freeing Israel from domination, he means only earthly Israel, and the domination to which he refers is only that of Rome. Jesus speaks of all people, the Romans included, as needing liberation, but he means being freed from sin and the suffering it causes. He is compassionate and humble, whereas Judas is certain his own way is the only way.'

'But Jesus said, "I am the Way, the Truth and the Light. No one comes to the Father but through me." '

'Yes, very good, but what did he mean?'

What? Kathy thought, having suddenly become con-fused. *Had he not meant exactly what he said?*

'Just that,' she said. 'He goes on to say, "He who believes in me will never die." '

'I don't think it's quite as simple as it sounds,' Michael continued, hoping he was not coming across as a know-it-all. ' "He who wishes to be my follower must deny his very self, take up his cross each day, and follow in my steps." '

'But how do we do that? We can't all be crucified!'

'No, but we must be willing to suffer for God or other people. We must give up everything else to serve Him wholeheartedly. "As I have done, so you must do." '

'What if we're never asked to give up everything or to suffer? How do we recognise God's will? Jesus was beyond temptation because he was better than we are. I don't care what Kazantzakis said. We can't be like him!'

'I believe it was absolutely necessary for Jesus to have been as enticed by what this life and this world offer as we are. I interpret the wilderness temptations not as having occurred only while Jesus was in the desert, but throughout his life. He had to have been completely human if his mission were to have any meaning. If he were the "firstborn of many", then I take that to imply we can, by his grace, conquer the temptations too. "He who has faith in me will do the things I've done, and greater far than these." If Jesus had not been wholly like us, but had been solely God, in the sense that God is above all weaknesses, then what he accomplished through leading a life free of sin would not have been such an awesome accomplishment.'

'Are you saying he wasn't God?' Kathy was shocked.

'No, I'm not saying that, but he was simultaneously fully human. Notice how several times Jesus is praying for God's will to be revealed to him. First, when he's talking to John the Baptist, the two disagree as to how mankind's redemption is to be achieved. The Baptist says God demands anger against all that's unjust. Jesus insists that love is enough. Later on, after he's had the revelations in the wilderness, Jesus realises the Baptist was correct. God spoke through John in order to instruct Jesus.'

'But since Jesus was God, why didn't he already know?'

'No fully human person is omniscient. How could God understand exactly what it is like to be a finite, fragile human being if he did not submit even to our limitations and restrictions?'

'Okay,' Kathy nodded, 'but what does the axe and chopping down the tree mean?'

'Do you remember Jesus's parable about the barren fruit tree? He said chop it down so that a more worthwhile tree could grow. This is a symbolic way of expressing that the evil must be destroyed so that the good may flourish. And later, returning to Jesus's humanity, when he's in Gethsemani, he's deeply distressed and afraid because of what will happen the next morning. He begs the Father to let the cup pass, to let redemption be achieved in a less painful way, but God lets His will be known when a disciple walks up and offers Jesus a cup of wine. All Jesus can rightfully do is accept and endure.'

'Why couldn't Jesus marry Magdalene? Why, since God knows everything, didn't God allow Jesus to wed her to keep her from turning to prostitution?'

'Jesus couldn't marry her. You know that.'

'But why? If it would have saved her ...'

'Who's to say it would have? She was saved anyway.'

Kathy sat back and reflected on Michael's words, on the latest images on the television screen. Having finished the novel, she was familiar with what was going on without having to watch it closely.

'But why would it have been such a sin for Jesus to have married and reared children? Near the end of the story it says: "harmony between the earth and the heart is the world of God." '

'Yes, but who says that? Satan says it. Jesus could not marry because the responsibilities of family life would

have prevented him from serving the Father as Jesus had
to do. He could not have roamed around preaching. His
duties to his family would have held him back from feeling
completely free to sacrifice himself.'

'Yes, but the book makes it seem a mortal sin for Jesus
to even dream about a normal life. That's the last
temptation, isn't it? What is Kazantzakis saying? Are all
people supposed to forego the ordinary life then?'

'Marrying and having children is not the right path for
everyone, but neither is giving up that type of life. I don't
understand all this, but I believe God has a certain reason
for wanting some people to marry and others to remain
celibate. Since we're all unique, God reaches out to us in
ways especially designed to touch our hearts and souls.
Apparently for most people family life is the best way to
accomplish this task; for others, and especially for Jesus
and for many other people, the so-called ordinary path of
marriage and childrearing, would have been a mortal
sin.'

'But why is sex such an evil? Why did God create sex
and give us bodies that desire it if it's a sin?'

'Sex is not a sin; it's a blessing. And it's not really the
most significant point of issue here. The question is more
concerned with submitting oneself to the will of God so
that He is free to mould you into who He means for you to
be.'

'Yet Jesus is especially ashamed of his sexual desires. He
lashes himself and begs forgiveness even for sexual dreams,
and those are involuntary and natural, supposedly. He
wants to sleep with women, particularly with Magdalene,
but he's afraid. He says he's afraid of everything? Why?
What does he fear? Do you think he has an unhealthy
attitude toward sex perhaps?'

Michael had to think more seriously about those questions.

'I think he's afraid of letting God down, and his is a grave responsibility. Think about it. The salvation of humankind rests solely on him. There's a cosmic balance of terror! At the period in his life when he says he's afraid of everything, before he's met John, or seen the visions in the desert, he's unsure of himself. He fears he may be an egotistical fool or a madman. No one understands him or the anguish he's suffering, not even his mother. It's curious how Kazantzakis made his Jesus a guilt-ridden Hamlet type. He can't make up his mind about anything either, and relies heavily on Judas's advice.'

'Do you think Jesus could've been like that?'

'I don't know! I've no idea. *Could've* been, yes. I definitely identify with this Jesus! When I first read this book I was profoundly inspired. You might say it changed my life.'

'Why do you identify with this Jesus?'

'I love God and want to serve Him, but I'm as confused and afraid as Kazantzakis made Jesus.'

'What are you afraid of?'

'I don't know exactly. I fear letting God down too, but I'm going to do that inevitably. I've done so more times than I know.'

'Catholic priests aren't allowed to marry, and so that's why you quit being a priest.' Kathy was certainly intuitive.

'Yes.' Michael's voice was barely audible.

'Why can't they marry? Baptist and Methodist preachers do; so do all the other types of preachers I've ever seen. Even Jewish rabbis can marry. I think they are almost required to take wives.'

'We believe a priest must devote himself completely to God's service. If he were married, he would have to give parts of himself to his family and livelihood.'

'But our preacher is dedicated to his church and to his

family. There's no problem.'

Michael did not want to be rude and say he disagreed with her. It was true that many Protestant clergymen loved and served the Lord well, but only in a manner of speaking. *They were evangelists, not priests! Oh, Lord, forgive me!* Michael prayed tacitly.

' "If anyone comes to me without turning his back on his father and mother, his wife and children, his brothers and sisters, indeed his very self, he cannot be my follower." ' Michael quoted finally, hoping Kathy would understand.

'Who said that?' She was appalled.

'Jesus.'

'But that sounds so cruel! How could he tell us to "love one another" and also say "turn your back on your family"?'

'In the movie, as we've seen, Mary, Jesus's mother, cannot understand her son. She wishes he were more like other young men. Finally Jesus will not even recognise her as his parent. Instead, he thinks of all people as his mother and father, and sisters and brothers. We must love all people equally. We're all God's children.'

'Kazantazkis does not believe in the Virgin birth, does he? And if we must love everyone the same, why shouldn't it also mean we must love all men as our husbands and all women as our wives? What would be the difference?'

'Lord! Lord! Lord!' Michael moaned to himself.

He remained quiet for a long time.

Kathy could not stand the silence.

'How do you feel about birth control and abortion?'

Michael leaned back in his chair.

'I haven't reached a final decision about abortion. It may be permissible under certain conditions, but if abortion is used by promiscuous people to rid themselves of the unwanted consequences of their actions, then it's definitely wrong. I have no problem with birth control, especially when used by a married couple who already have children.'

'What about between the unmarried?' Kathy ventured also to ask, feeling unusually bold.

'Again, if people use birth control as a means to get by with promiscuous behaviour, it's wrong.'

'What, in your opinion, is promiscuous behaviour?'

'I mean that sex is promiscuous when it's done merely for the pleasure it can give, or going to bed with someone you don't know well.'

'How long must two people know each other first?'

'I can't answer such a question.' Michael wondered where all these questions were leading. 'Some people seem to have known each other for years only after they've just met. Others may not know each other well even after they've dated for six months. I do feel, however, that if two people truly love one another, they should be willing to wait however long it may take until they are sure they are ready for the intimacies of sex. Love making must happen naturally, in the fullness of time.'

'But what about those people you mentioned who seemed to have known each other for ever right after they first met?'

'Though they may feel they've known each other for ever, that doesn't mean they should immediately fall into bed. Their relationship must be built up, like a gradual unfolding of the mysteries of each aspect of their personalities. They must develop a mutual respect and appreciation for each other as vital, multi-faceted individuals. It makes the love making experience better when it finally does happen. You must regard the sexual sharing as a spiritual experience, and not merely as a fleshly commingling. If the pleasure is all you're after, then it's all you're going to get, if you even get it. There's much more to be

108

experienced than the excitements of the body alone. If all you want is the fleshly pleasure, then you're lusting; you're treating your partner as a sexual object. You're being selfish and beastly. In time, you may discover the pleasure is not even the best part of the activity.'

'What else could there be?'

Kathy was on a roll; her audacity surprised her and she enjoyed it.

'Just being in such proximity to your beloved ... and if you regard sexuality as a mystical practice, you may eventually be awed by what you'll discover. The Hindus have a discipline called *kundalini*. If practised patiently for years, one may attain marvellous revelations about God, the Cosmos, and the natures of life and death. In good love making you reach a point at which you forget your ego-self entirely; it's as though you suddenly and briefly become one with your partner, and one with all of creation.'

'But then it's over, right?'

'No, you recall the feeling of unity and through it you may gradually discover greater insights. Everything and everyone in the universe are interrelated, and all contain God and are contained by God. God is both transcendant and immanent simultaneously.'

Kathy's spiel had run its course. Michael's words had awed her once again.

'How were you able to leave the priesthood and marry, since you love God so much?'

Michael looked at her, studying her expression. She seemed after him markedly this night. *Why?* But her questions were apt.

'I thought I had misunderstood God's will for me by becoming a priest,' he said simply.

'Did you?' Kathy moved to a spot beside him on the couch.

109

'I don't know yet.'

'How do we know what God's will is?' she asked.

Damn good question! Michael thought. He had wrestled with it for years and had finally come across an answer in Thomas Merton's *New Seeds of Contemplation*. Now he strained to recall the gist of it.

'Thomas Merton said something like: "to consent to God's will is to consent to be true, or to speak truth, or at least to seek it. To obey God is to respond to His will expressed in the need of another person, or at least to respect the rights of others . . . If I am supposed to hoe a graden or make a table, then I am obeying God if I am true to the task I am performing." '

Additional reading in St Teresa of Avila, Joseph Campbell, Alan Watts, St Augustine, the *Bhagavad Gita*, Julian of Norwich and St John of the Cross had further convinced him, as had the Bible.

'So, doing our best at whatever each day gives us to do is the will of God.'

'That's part of it, but there's more, I believe. Doing our best for the love of God is no more than a duty. We must go beyond what's expected. First we must give ourselves to God, for we have nothing else He could want, and we should tell Him we're ready and eager to endure whatever He might ask.'

Michael stopped; he was suddenly confused again. This line of conversation had touched too many sensitive nerves. Now he felt like a presumptuous fool. *What did he know?* His head started throbbing and he had become weary. *There was yet so much he did not comprehend*! The smallest movement was now an arduous struggle. He was exhausted by all the years of striving and fighting. Diverse images flickered through his mind, choppylike, unnatural, like those filmed with a hand-cranked movie camera in the silent screen era. An ethereal soprano floated in from above the air and hovered hummingbird-like near a flower. *Could Kathy hear it?* he wondered. *How absurd the image was!* Michael looked at her; his behaviour had startled her.

'Oh Kathy, I don't know what the hell I'm talking about now!'

He felt like a failure. He was a traitor as Jesus had been in the last temptation nightmare. Suddenly depressed and light years away in mind, Michael retreated into himself. *Was Kathy an ox goad and he the ox,* he mused. *Who had sent her? God or Satan? Could she possibly be to him what the negro boy in the novel, the beautiful girl in the movie, had been to the Jesus who came down from the cross? Who, what had Angela been? And, for that matter, who and what was he to Angela and Kathy?* He was not better than they. He feared the foundation of a lifetime's painfully developed philosphical system had suddenly collapsed. *What had been his foundation then?* he asked himself. *If it had been God, it would not have crumbled. What mattered any more?*

Ever so delicately Kathy moved closer, embraced Michael, and gently kissed him. She sensed his anguish and wanted to offer comfort.

What she did not comprehend was that the consolation she offered was not the kind he required. Michael had reached a point in his spiritual maturation at which God alone could suffice. What did Kathy know of Michael's "dark night"? Though Michael knew intellectually that God alone could suitably comfort him, emotionally he had yet to be finally convinced. 'The spirit is willing, but the flesh is weak,' he recalled. He wanted to accept and singleheartedly appreciate Kathy's embrace and kisses, and momentarily he surrendered.

Kathy made the most of the situation. Though she was relatively new to such behaviour, she had taken clues from the movies and from romance novels. Michael kissed her

111

repeatedly on the lips and throat, feverishly, hungrily, and his hands quickly found their way into her clothing. All else was forgotten for the moment. Tantalising Kathy, he roamed his hands over the contours of her breasts, back and hips, drawing her on top of him as they reclined. Tenaciously pressing herself against his body, as if desiring to absorb him, she allowed her hands to do their own explorations. It was frightening how anxiously she yearned to possess him completely.

'Make love to me!' she breathed hoarsely, clutching at him. 'Please!'

Violently extracting himself from contact with her, Michael exclaimed, 'No, Kathy, we can't do this! It's wrong, wrong!'

'Why?'

Kathy demanded that he explain his reasons to her, both disappointed and angry.

'I love you, don't you know that?'

'You *can't* love me!' he insisted.

He bewildered her.

'What is that supposed to mean?'

'I have no right to you.'

'I believe you have whatever rights I choose to give you. I've chosen you, can't you see?'

'But I can't. It wouldn't be proper.'

'Why? Tell me why.'

Why? Michael demanded of himself, now doubly confused. *Because ... because we're surrendering to temporal pleasures that are made only of mist.* 'For the moth doth corrupt, and the thief breaketh in and stealeth,' he recalled. *Because God alone can ultimately satisfy. We're accepting substitutes, which are incomplete in themselves, instead of seeking only after God's premium.*

"Since true devotion comes from the heart and looks only to the truth and substance represented by spiritual

112

objects, and since everything else is imperfect attachment and possessiveness, any appetite for these things must be uprooted if some degree of perfection is to be reached," St John of the Cross had written in *Dark Night of the Soul*.

Michael sat trembling for over five minutes after moving away from Kathy. He could quote numerous other authors with regard to this type of circumstance, and though he felt they had all been correct, he still could not completely understand why. Though he had earlier denied that sex was the issue, it was, even if Michael did not know precisely why. *What would be so wrong if we made love? Damn it!* he cursed. *I need to resolve this dilemma!*

'Michael, you are no longer a priest,' Kathy said calmly. Her flash of anger had dissipated. 'I am not merely a student who has developed a crush on her teacher. I think about you all the time, and want only to be with you. Forgive me, but I thought you shared some of my feelings.'

'I do,' he said quietly and honestly. 'But I couldn't. You're too young for me.'

'I don't care how old you are. You're more attractive than any boy I know, and far more interesting. You're mature and sensitive; most of the boys my age are silly. All they think about are sports, sex and getting drunk.'

'Sex has been much on your mind tonight.'

'No, making love has. There's a difference, as I'm sure you're well aware.'

He was indeed, but would little expect a twenty-year-old to know also.

'Michael, I do love you, and I want to be as close to you as it's possible. I'm sorry if I've misread your feelings all along. I guess you have no interest in making love with me.'

Gently he took her face in his hands, gazed into her eyes and kissed her tenderly.

'Believe me, I do. I want to make love to you so much that I'm trembling inside. I just can't.'

'Is there a physical impairment preventing it?' she asked quietly.

'No, it's nothing like that. "I fled Him, down the nights and down the days; I fled Him, down the labyrinthine ways of my own mind; and in the mist of tears I hid from Him ... from those strong Feet that followed ... with unhurrying chase ... and a voice beat more instant than the feet – all things betray thee, who betrayest Me." '

Michael feelingly recited from Francis Thompson's poem, *The Hound of Heaven*.

'What are you talking about?'

Kathy was exasperated with him. *Was Michael absolutely crazy?*

' "For though I knew His love Who followed, yet was I sore adread lest having Him, I must have naught else beside ... Nature, poor stepdame, cannot slake my drouth; Let her, if she would owe me, drop yon blue-bosom veil of sky and show me, the breasts o' her tenderness ... Lo! Naught contents thee, who content'st Me." '

Misunderstanding the poem, Kathy slipped out of her sweater, unbuttoned her blouse, and exposed her breasts to Michael. Though he looked on their ample loveliness with wondrous admiration, he felt no more lust.

' "All which I took from thee",' Michael continued, ' "I did but take not for thy harms, but just that thou might'st seek it in My arms. All which they child's mistake fancies as lost, I have stored for thee at home. Rise, clasp My hand, and come ... I am He whom thou seekest! Thou dravest love from thee, who dravest Me." '

'I don't understand what you're saying.'

'That's a poem, Kathy, about how God is unrelenting in His drawing of a soul to Himself. We can rebel and run and try to hide all we want, but He will not give up.'

'I don't think most people experience things like that, Michael. I know I never have. I've never known anyone who has.'

'It's always been just that way with me. I've felt God near me all my life. He's had His hand on me and He will not remove it. I've tried to make him go away, but He won't. In the novel, remember, Jesus always heard voices and footsteps shuffling after him. It's been the same with me.'

'Are you saying you're like Jesus?'

Michael sighed,

'I don't know! I am similar to Kazantzakis's portrait of Jesus anyway. That doesn't mean I am special or better than anyone else, but only that perhaps I see life quite differently than most people. I don't know how other people see life exactly, but as you said, they do not seem to have such experiences, or if they do, they ignore them because they have no idea what they mean. Forgive me, please, but I've not been able to resolve these conflicts.'

'How can I help you? I want to help if I can,' Kathy said with sincere concern and rebuttoned her blouse.

Michael smiled,

'Thank you, but I don't know if you can help me. I sense it's only between God and myself. Your concern means worlds to me. Please bear with me.'

'I'm sorry for behaving as I did.' Kathy was ashamed now. 'I'll wait. I'll be patient.'

'When the time is right, we'll both know.' Slowly Michael got up, flipped off the TV and VCR, and went into the kitchen.

Kathy sat still for a while considering Michael's words. When she glanced at her watch she was shocked to learn it was 1.15.

'Oh no! Michael!' She jumped up. 'It's after one! I

can't get into the dorm now.'

For a few minutes Michael studied the latest development.

'You can sleep in my room. I'll take the sofa,' he said, leaning against the doorpost between the kitchen and living room.

'Are you mad at me?''

'Why should I be?'

'I wouldn't feel right taking your bed. You sleep there and I'll take the sofa.'

'No, don't worry about it.'

As if to close the motion, Michael set down his bottle of mineral water and started gathering pillows and blankets to make the sofa more comfortable.

'I don't suppose you have an extra toothbrush?'

Kathy was fastidious, and could not bear the thought of going to bed without cleaning her teeth.

'Yes, as a matter of fact, I do,' Michael said, and went into the bathroom and brought Kathy one he had not yet opened.

While Kathy performed her nightly routines, Michael laid out for her a pair of his pyjamas.

Later, after showering and brushing his teeth, Michael lay awake on the couch for hours; he had much to think about. Reviewing the evening's events, he criticised his words and actions, wondering how he might better have handled the situation. Angela was also in his thoughts more than usual; he still missed her dearly and recalled all the plans they had made. He was tempted to go to Kathy, but forced the notion out of his mind.

Kathy could not sleep either, and she wished Michael would change his mind and join her in bed. Though he might not feel prepared for greater intimacies, a fact that surprised her (having been led to believe all her life that men were always eager for sex), Kathy was certain she

116

was more than ready. Nevertheless, she tried to respect his decision. Lying in Michael's bed, wearing his flannel pyjamas, Kathy delighted in his scent which lingered in them, and pondered the situation. *How was it possible Michael, just in the next room, with no one to know or care what they did, was yet unwilling to seize the opportunity so freely offered to him? Would she ever understand his sentiments?* She felt helpless and sick at heart; she could not have described her feelings if she had been asked to do so. *He was only in the next room! She could go in and touch him! What if he became angry though?* Fearing his rejection, wanting to cry, Kathy suppressed her tears; she did not want to annoy him further.

10

The final two weeks of Fall semester were, as usual, extremely busy. Everyone rushed about tensely, nervously, preoccupied; it was an exciting but stressful time. Because of a performance of Mozart's *Requiem* on the fifth, the first week of December was especially tiring for Kathy. Michael was sure to attend the show at the Hutchin's Concert Hall to show his support for her. This Requiem was one of his favourite Masses. As he listened to the chamber choir's performance, he relaxed, allowing his imagination to be charged.

As Michael listened to the first movement, he saw a giant with monstrously large feet walking ponderously across a stone floor. All seemed to be shadowy, sombre, spooky. It was Goliath, or the giant from *Jack, the Giant Killer* or maybe it was Wotan, the Germanic god, in Valhalla. Perhaps Zeus was angry. Then a crystal soprano, Kathy's in fact, floated in from heaven. It was the feminine nature attempting to calm and quieten the masculine. Michael contemplated the Jungian anima and animus, and then realised he had died.

Fearfully he shuffled up a long staircase. It was narrow and miraculously spanned the chasm between earth and heaven; it reminded Michael of a suspended rope bridge. Maybe it was Jacob's ladder. His heart repeatedly beat *kyrie eleison* and the soprano soothed his fears. Though he could not hear all of her words well enough to understand precisely what she was saying, because of the pounding in his head, he was comforted by them. Maybe the woman was his mother encouraging him to persevere. Maybe the voice belonged to the Madonna herself. The rest of the angelic choir echoed with *kyrie eleison*; they were undoubtedly made up of all the saints and they were interceding on his behalf. *Hell, Mozart never saw all this, did he? Hold on, man, no need to freak out here. I'm a nutcase!* Michael mused to himself, amazed at all the phantoms embedded in his mind, all the diverse, often bizarre images.

On the *Dies Irae*, the Day of Wrath, Michael cowered before the judgement bench of the Almighty. In this nightmare God had the aspect more of an irate Zeus than of a gentle shepherd. It was disconcerting, and Michael became more terrified at the thought of what such a capricious deity might do to him. He saw the mad Caligula from Robert Graves's *I, Claudius* and started trembling. In the *Lacrimosa*, the Lament, Michael wept and begged for the Lord's mercy, knowing clearly he deserved none. *Just give me a reprieve then! I've said all I can. It's up to You now*, he said finally and bowed his head.

During the *Sanctus*, the Holy, Michael truly imagined peculiar sights. The saints were now performing a quirky music hall or Broadway routine in which they wore straw summer hats, natty blue blazers and white pants, and carried canes. First they danced onto a stage following one another, and in turn each one would sing parts of the prayer in their effort to convince God to be merciful. *Now this is really weird!* Michael thought, shaking his head.

Finally during the *Lux Aeterna*, the Eternal Light, Michael glimpsed the loving saviour. Jesus sat with cherubim children all around him, as Michael had seen depicted in numerous paintings. With indescribable relief Michael knew he had been forgiven and accepted into the kingdom. The choir closed with Mozart's *Laudate Dom-*

inum, and Michael envisioned paradise in the guise of an earlier era of history when life was less complicated. *No such era ever really existed,* he corrected himself. *That is an ephemeral daydream.* During all this music Michael sensed Mozart had been concocting a final joke, even though he knew the composer had been in bad health and was suffering from great debts during the *Requiem's* composition. Nevertheless, all he saw now were the sillier antics of the boy in the film *Amadeus.*

Needless to say, Michael enjoyed the Chamber Singers' performance immensely. It lightened his mood and gave him a stress-free respite during the frenzy of the last few days of the semester. A week ago he and Kathy had watched *The Last Temptation of Christ,* and had gotten carried away with those other activities. It seemed to have been a month ago. About three weeks until Christ's Mass, Michael realised. It had sneaked up on him again this year. Now it was only the religious significance of Christmas that meant anything to him, since he had no family. He did delight in the friendliness and excitement he observed in other people, but he despised the commercialism. *Do most people take the time to contemplate what they're celebrating?* he wondered. Michael looked forward to the Christmas Eve mass, the Vigil; the traditional readings, hymns, the bellringing, the poinsettias, the selections from the *Roman Martyrology*: these always moved him to tears of joy and thanksgiving.

During the next week Michael and Kathy had hardly any time to spend together. It was only on the eighteenth of December, during final exams week, that they found leisure enough. Kathy would be flying home on Saturday, and they both wanted to see each other first.

'I want to be with you all the time,' Kathy admitted.

Michael stared at the floor. He was thankful to hear those words, but still feared what all they could mean.

120

'I wish I didn't have to go home. I'd rather stay here with you,' Kathy continued.

'Don't be silly! You'll have a much better time with your family. Don't you miss them? You've not seen any of them for over four months!'

'I know, and yes, I do miss them, but I'll miss you even more. I'll think of you here in this beautiful, but bitterly cold, white world, all alone, nowhere to go. What will you do? What kind of holiday will you have?'

'I have friends. I have my church. There's lots to do.'

'You mean you have Rudy and Mark?'

'Yes, and Jacob. He has a large family, and I'm always invited to their parties.'

'But he's Jewish. Jews don't celebrate Christmas.'

'Jacob's mother and wife are both Christians, so they do celebrate Christmas. It's always a grand affair too. They have lots of friends and relatives. I won't be alone, don't worry.'

'I still don't want to leave you.'

'Are you sure?'

'Absolutely.'

'Do you have to go? Would your parents understand?'

'No,' she admitted sadly, 'they definitely would not understand. I haven't told them about you, except that you're my favourite teacher.'

'It would hurt them, wouldn't it? No doubt they have been making big plans for your visit.'

She nodded.

'Then you must go. I'll be fine. I want you to forget about me and enjoy being with them. They deserve it. You'll get to see your cat Jonathan, and Candy.'

Kathy smiled at the thought of seeing Jonathan and Candy again. Maybe it wouldn't be too chilly in Georgia and she could go for a ride on the horse. No doubt her grandmother and mother would bake homemade cookies;

Kathy would be sure to bring back some to Michael.

On Saturday Michael drove Kathy to the Bangor International Airport and saw her off. Immediately afterwards he drove over to the mall to do his Christmas shopping. Yes, it was late in the season, he admitted, and the stores were almost as crowded as the hallways of a grammar school when the bell rang for class change, but Michael enjoyed the decorations, the carols and the delight he saw in peoples' faces. Deciding on a gift for Kathy was a most thoughtful undertaking, and he had purchased everyone else's present before he made up his mind.

On Christmas Eve Michael acted as deacon in the mass at St Luke's. The church was packed, as was usual for major celebrations, and many people had to stand. It was immensely joyful to feel the church shake as all of them sang "Hark the Herald Angels Sing" for the opening hymn. Very happily Michael walked in the procession through the central aisle; he felt whole and at peace. Mark, though not a Catholic, attended this service. Afterward the two of them went to Mark's rented duplex and stayed up late talking. Mark had no family to visit either. Though he had been married and divorced, he and his wife were not on good terms. He would have loved to see his son, now twenty-two years old, but he had neither the money nor the energy to make the long trip to Florida. Key West was Mark's home town; he was a thoroughbred "conch", and though he loved visiting there, he was not able to do so except during the summer vacations. Then he despised the resort atmosphere the island had fallen prey to during the last thirty-odd years. It was not quite his home any longer due to all the tourists and the hype, and the prices for basic commodities had become exorbitant. The natives of Key West, especially the elderly, such as his octogenarian ailing parents, were suffering dearly.

Mark helped them out as much as he could, but at fifty-three, and with illnesses of his own, he was feeling his age more and more. Michael's friendship was much cherished by Mark; he considered Michael a soul-mate. Their life views were incredibly similar, and they could sit for hours conversing profoundly about philosophy, literature, psychology, mysticism, and any other subject. Both were widely read, Renaissance men, and each had learned much from the other. Michael frequently thought of Mark as a guru, and it would have surprised him to learn that Mark thought likewise of him.

On Christmas Day, after Mass, Michael went over to Jacob's house. As usual, Jacob put on a lavish celebration. Three generations of his family were gathered into the large, colourfully decorated house, and foods of every description enticed one with their aromas and titillating displays. Michael especially enjoyed the traditional feast; they all sat around a massive oak table in Jacob's formal dining room, just like in a Norman Rockwell painting. Michael was treated as a member of the family, and the children particularly adored him. He took the time to play games with them, and treated them as equals. After the meal they opened gifts and sang Christmas carols with Jacob at the piano.

During the next week Michael drove down to Portland, did some shopping in the after-Christmas sales, and stopped off at the outlet stores in Freeport on his way back home. During the following few days he did much reading, watching old movies on television with Mark, (it seemed every channel had to show *It's a Wonderful Life* at least ten times!), and on one day was persuaded to go with Rudy and his girlfriend Cassie ice-skating. When in solitude Michael tried to meditate, but he started missing Kathy increasingly. He needed to come to terms about his relationship with her, but he did not know how. While rereading Alan Watts' *Nature, Man and Woman*, he re-evaluated the way he had been thinking. He loved her, he really did, and she had said she loved him. Their love for each other should sanctify their relationship, as the love between Angela and himself had done. *Where had he gotten such psychologically unhealthy guilt feelings regarding sexual attraction?* He was not lusting after Kathy; his desires to make love with her were natural because of their feelings for each other. He had no intention of using her; he loved all of her, and was not attracted solely to her body. Talking with her, sharing ideas, witnessing her discoveries, her wonder, these meant worlds to him, and there was so much more he hoped to share with her. *Were these feelings wrong?* he asked, not wanting to think about the ethical questions now; he did not want to think about them at all. For a while at least, he hoped to be happy again, to stop feeling he was fighting a battle he would inevitably lose anyway. Although Michael loved God deeply, striving constantly to please Him could depress a person and make him grim. Michael did not want to be an unpleasant person for others to be around; he wanted to feel fully alive again, and he believed Kathy could help him. *She said she wanted to help, didn't she?* he asked, trying to decide if he had understood what she meant.

Michael was watching television when Kathy showed up smiling at his door. She had returned three days earlier than planned because she missed him so much. Forgetting all lingering reservations, Michael heartily embraced her.

'I don't know what I'm going to do with you,' he said with a smile and ushered her inside.

'What do you mean?' she asked with her own large smile. 'Do you care for me or not?'

She carried a colourful holiday cookie tin and a red and green wrapped package.

Michael stared intently into her eyes, weighing the

options, reviewing all the thoughts he had had during the last two weeks.

'I love you.'

Kathy grinned and said excitedly, 'Let's leave here. Let's go to your cabin where no one will bother us. We won't tell anyone where we're going. We have over a week before the new semester begins.'

Michael brightened at her suggestion.

'I'll go get a few items from my room. Meet me in the parking lot beside the dormitory in an hour. You pack your bags too.'

'Are you sure?' Michael asked uncertainly.

'Yes, I'm positive.'

'You'd better bring your warmest clothes.'

'Yes, all right.'

Michael could not explain what crazy idea compelled him to pack as much as he did. They had only nine days after all, but Michael wanted to take along all the books and musical recordings, all the films, that he and Kathy could ever need; there was such a lot he wanted to share with her. It was true there were many already at the cabin, but some of his favourites needed to be taken along. Clothes meant little to him, and he had more at the cabin than in Orono, but Michael made sure he included his best jeans and sweaters. Feeling rather silly, he placed all these items in every carrying case he possessed and loaded the Ranger's bed. For the moment he laid a tarpaulin loosely over them.

Kathy's packing was as excessive as Michael's, in its own way. She too included her favourite clothing, even a nice dress – *in case there was an elegant party out in the backwoods*! *Yeah right*! She chided her lunacy, but packed the dress anyway. Taking along her satchel of school-books, making sure Michael's *Bhagavad-Gita* was inside, and items no woman could possibly do without, she was

125

ready to go. Michael arrived to pick her up punctually, helped her place her suitcase in the truck, and tied the tarp down securely. Before heading out of town they stopped at a grocery store to buy provisions.

Light snow was falling again as they left Orono, but the highway department was ready if situations should worsen. Kathy admired the tranquil-looking farmhouses, all wrapped in snow like a Currier and Ives painting on a Christmas card. Kathy felt wholesome inside; the feeling was perfect. She was so glad she had decided to come back to Maine early. Eagerly she looked forward to arriving at the cabin; she was anxious to see it. Meanwhile she enjoyed the New England landscapes and thought they did not differ much from some of those of Georgia, except for the snow.

'Do we have some hot chocolate?' she asked, wishing she had thought to buy some at the grocery store. 'Can we stop in the next town to get some?'

'There's some at the cabin already.'

'Oh good! We must have a cup when we get there. We'll sit in front of a glowing, crackling fire, sip our cocoa, open our presents and talk. It will seem very domestic. Let's roast some hot dogs too. They can be our dinner.'

It was after eight when they arrived. The cabin was slightly larger than Kathy expected. For reasons which were not clear to her, she thought of Teddy Roosevelt. There were no moose or deer heads adorning the walls, no safari hats or shotguns, but if there had been she would not have been surprised. The cabin's rustic simplicity immediately attracted her and made her feel at ease. Very few pieces of furniture were painted; most were stained or varnished. Point and Chief Joseph Indian blankets were draped across the chairs and sofa, and the walls were made of logs and mortar. If anything was painted at all, the colours were invariably foresty green, burnt red or earthy brown. Books were everywhere, even more than at the apartment in Orono, and notebooks filled with essays, stories and journals Michael had written over the years were neatly shelved alongside the bound volumes. On the wall above the mantle hung a hand-crafted crucifix; Michael's grandfather had carved it when Michael was born. There was a television, a VCR and many video-tapes, but the reception was so bad the TV was only useful for viewing tapes. Michael had an extensive LP and cassette collection, and had begun a CD library too; Kathy was impressed with the range of his tastes.

Her bedroom was cosy. A beautiful quilt covered the bed, and had it been daylight she would have been transfixed by the vistas outside the window. After bringing in their luggage, Michael went about his customary routines of lighting a fire, plugging in the refrigerator, turning up the gas heat, and checking out everything, making sure all was as it should be. Kathy leisurely unpacked her things, wanting to make her surroundings as homey as possible. The cute stuffed Sharpei dog a friend had given her for Christmas gave her bedroom the perfect touch. Very neatly Kathy arranged her clothes and personal items in the drawers and closet of her room; she laid out her brush and comb, her perfumes, deodorant, the few types of makeup she used, her lotion, shampoo, toothbrush, and Colgate paste. Everything had its place; Kathy was meticulously orderly. And though she was well aware of the briefness of her residency here, she wanted to create an illusion of permanence.

After satisfying herself with the situation of her room, she went through the rest of the cabin acquainting herself with it. The bathroom was Victorian; its bathtub had lion paw feet. Michael had decorated all the house, and the bathroom had not been neglected. The shower curtain was blue with butterflies on it, and complemented the half-panelled, half-wallpapered walls. The design was flowery, spring-like, and cheerful. Checking out Michael's bedroom, Kathy ran her hands over the red silk-backed quilt on his bed. On the night stand she noticed a copy of Jean-Paul Sartre's autobiography, *The Words*, and a New Testament. Hanging on the bedpost was Michael's black Greek fisherman's cap; she had not seen him wearing it lately, but thought he looked roguishly masculine when he did. He ought to wear Old Spice cologne, she mused, whenever he was going to don that cap. It never occurred to Kathy to wonder if Michael would care for her to be nosing around in his room; she felt completely comfortable around him, as if they had been together for fifteen years. Though he had a crucifix in his bedroom, Michael also had a statue of the Buddha, and scented candles set on each side of it as if it were a shrine. She wondered about that. Since the closet door was open, Kathy sifted through his clothes. They smelled of him, and she enjoyed his scent.

Moving back downstairs, Kathy went into the kitchen. A counter separated it from the living room. She was astonished by the sight of the stove. It appeared to be ancient to her eyes.

'What do you think?' Michael asked, coming back inside, his arms loaded with wood.

'I love it!' She smiled gleefully. 'It's very cosy and relaxing. I can already understand why you love it here.'

As he walked over to the fireplace he said, 'Is your room suitable?'

'Oh, yes. That quilt is beautiful. Did your mother make it?'

'No, I bought it in Pennsylvania,' he admitted, and proceeded to the fireplace to lay down the extra wood.

'Michael, how does that stove work?'

It was a 1930 vintage Sears Peerless Combination coal

and gas range. If natural gas were not available, anything that would burn could be used for fuel. Michael returned to the kitchen and demonstrated the stove's features and showed her how to work it. Kathy thought it might not be so bad after all (as long as she did not have to worry about cooking over an open fire).

'It's very old, isn't it?'

'Yeah, about sixty years, I think.'

Michael turned on the gas and lit up a burner to put a kettle on to boil.

'I'm ready for some hot chocolate, how about you?'

'Yeah!' Kathy exclaimed, recalling how much she had craved some earlier.

While waiting for the water to boil, Kathy explored the kitchen's cabinets and pantry. She quickly located the Swiss Miss hot chocolate with marshmallows. There were also lots of canned goods of all varieties, boxes of Carnation evaporated milk, various types of herbal tea, peanut butter, spices of every description, plentiful types of pasta (in canisters made from emptied jars of Classico spaghetti sauce just like at the apartment), potatoes, onions, dried beans and peas, and staples such as corn meal, flour and sugar. With the additional fresh bread, fruits, vegetables, and several types of meat they had bought in Orono, they were in fine shape food wise. He had sufficient cooking utensils, pots, skillets and dishes; Kathy was satisfied.

When the teapot whistled Michael got two mugs from the cabinet; Kathy had already laid out two Swiss Miss packets.

'Come on!' she squealed with excitement. 'It's time you opened your Christmas presents!'

Always the type to take things leisurely, Michael took the time to set a mood. The fire was glowing by now; snow was falling; the cabin was warm throughout; all they needed now was music. He considered what selection to make, and decided Pachelbel's *Canon* would do nicely. Upon witnessing the bouncy jubilance of Kathy's reaction, he knew he had chosen wisely. She had heard it before, but had not known what it was.

'Here!' she said, thrusting a package at him.

Michael handed her the gifts he had gotten for her, but she insisted he open his first. One was the compact disc recording of Paul McCartney's *Liverpool Oratorio*; Kathy had remembered Michael telling her how awed he had been after watching a television presentation of it in late October. Michael was thrilled by the gift, but felt she had spent too much money on it. When he tasted Kathy's mother's homemade chocolate chip biscuits he remarked honestly that they reminded him of his mother's. Next he forced Kathy to open her gifts; he was as excited as she was. One was a recording of Gabrielli's *Regina Coeli*; he had found it finally in Portland. Another was a turquoise-inlaid Celtic cross, and the last a bound anthology of English poetry. Kathy had never had a happier Christmas and she hugged Michael effusively.

'Can we listen to the Gabrielli now?' she asked politely.

Michael could not have been more assured of her gratitude. Pachelbel was finished anyway, and the sombre adagio of Albinoni-Giazotto was now playing. McCartney could wait. Michael loved the *Regina Coeli* too.

'Shall we roast the hot dogs now?' he wondered as the music started. He was hungry.

Kathy slept peacefully that night, and the celestial notes of Gabrielli's hymn to the Queen of Heaven meandered through her dreams. She was consummately happy and perfectly at ease. When she awoke to the bright, sunny but cold morning, she was full of zeal and excitement, and eager to take a leisurely walk. Michael had already prepared breakfast, and had long been up and about. His mood was chipper.

After Kathy had eaten, she and Michael took a hike through the woods. Kathy revelled as much in the wilderness as Michael, and they sat and watched a herd of deer for ten minutes. All throughout the day Michael studied her intently. It felt natural for them to be together as they were. *Could I marry her?* he wondered. *She possesses a natural, unaffected grace,* he thought as he watched her. Her long, glossy dark hair was tied in a ponytail, accentuating her high cheekbones. *Maybe she's a Cherokee Indian princess!*

Totally absorbed by her wonder in the forest, occasionally glimpsing a wild animal, Kathy did not realise she was such an object of scrutiny. Michael had always loved the way she dressed; she had a unique style all her own. Although she was very much a modern woman, she favoured dressing in long, flowery, Polynesian-type skirts, or conservative Scottish plaids, or maybe jeans that flattered her trim, shapely figure. In warmer weather, as in the autumn, she preferred huaraches or other sandals; now she wore more practical calf-high leather boots. Kathy also liked to add splashes of colour with bead belts, scarves and hats. As Angela had possessed, Kathy too had a vibrant flair; it was artistic and inherently complementary to her personality.

During the last four months Michael had enjoyed watching Kathy discover herself; she was not as shy as she had been, not as hesitant to speak up. In class at first she hardly said anything; by the second half of the semester she was one of the most prominent questioners and commentators. She had required only a gentle push, for she was truly an extraordinary young woman. What would she be in ten years? he wondered, and wished he could still know her then.

When they returned to the cabin, Kathy took up her anthology of English poetry. Curling up on the sofa before the fireplace, she started reading. The Romantics put her

131

in an even more contented mood. Michael joined her with a book too, and from time to time would share favourite verses with her. Quite distinct from Kathy's romantic reverie, Michael was perusing the *Duino Elegies* of Rilke.

Who, if I cried out, would hear me among the angels'
hierarchies? and even if one of them pressed me
suddenly against his heart: I would be consumed
in that overwhelming existence.

Not that you could endure
God's voice – far from it. But listen to the voice of the wind
and the ceaseless message that forms itself out of silence.

He read in the first elegy, and Rilke's words echoed some of Michael's own more recent thoughts. It was not that Michael's faith in God was in jeopardy, but that he felt he had forgotten how to be alive because of his ultimately futile attempts to be "good". Michael had been trying to be more than he was, to live up to an ideal that was not humanly possible. Any religion which tried to deny the humanity of its adherents was of doubtful merit, Michael now believed. Jesus celebrated the good-ness in people, in life itself; he did not go around, like some clerical types Michael knew, with a reproving look in his eyes. Some of the Existentialist poet's words reminded Michael also of those of Camus. Michael read on in Rilke's fourth elegy:

I won't endure these half-filled human masks;
better, the puppet. It at least is full.
I'll put up with the stuffed skin, the wire, the face
that is nothing but appearance.

The seventh elegy took Michael completely out of

himself.

Truly being here is glorious. Even you knew it,
you girls who seemed to be lost, to go under---, in the
filthiest
streets of the city, festering there, or wide open
for garbage. For each of you had an hour, or perhaps
not even an hour, a barely measurable time
between two moments---, when you were granted a sense
of being. Everything. Your veins flowed with being.
But we can so easily forget what our laughing neighbour
neither confirms nor envies. We want to display it,
to make it visible, though even the most visible happiness
can't reveal itself to us until we transform it, within.

He skipped over to the tenth elegy, which was another
of his favourites.

How dear you will be to me then, you nights
of anguish. Why didn't I kneel more deeply to accept you,
inconsolable sisters, and surrendering, lose myself
in your loosened hair. How we squander our hours of
pain.
How we gaze beyond them into the bitter duration
to see if they have an end.

The Law of Pathe Mathos: "Zeus, whose law it is that
he who learns must suffer" (Aeschylus, *Agamemnon*), was
taught by Rilke also, it seemed to Michael. *How many
different places had he come across this lesson in his reading and in
his own experience?*
At 4.30 Kathy began to prepare the meal she had been
planning carefully. She put on a chicken to bake, stewed
potatoes, boiled corn on the cob, tossed a salad, and
stirred up the batter for homemade Southern cornbread.

133

Michael was given strict orders to stay out of her way, and he dutifully continued his reading. His attention, however, was increasingly broken by his renewed scrutiny of Kathy.

'You look sleepy,' Kathy observed as she relaxed while the chicken baked.

'Dreamy,' he responded.

'Why don't you nap while the dinner cooks? I'll call you when it's ready.'

'No, I'm fine.'

Michael thoroughly enjoyed Kathy's meal, and appreciated the effort she had made.

'What is your favourite poem by Wordsworth?' she asked later as they sat on the sofa again after eating.

He thought about the question a few minutes, and then said he was torn between *Tintern Abbey*, *Ode: Intimations of Immortality*, and parts of *The Prelude*.

'Read something to me,' Kathy said, and handed him the anthology.

Michael turned to *The Prelude*, and began to read:

"Oh there is blessing in this gentle breeze,
A visitant that while it fans my cheek
Doth seem half-conscious of the joy it brings
From the green fields, and from yon azure sky.
Whate'er it's mission, the soft breeze can come
To none more grateful than to me; escaped
From the vast city, where I long had pined
A discontented sojourner: now free.
Free as a bird to settle where I will.
What dwelling shall receive me? In what vale
Shall be my harbour? underneath what grove
Shall I take up my home? and what clear stream
Shall with its murmur lull me into rest?
The earth is all before me. With a heart

Joyous, nor scared at its own liberty,
I look about; and should the chosen guide
Be nothing better than a wandering cloud,
I cannot miss my way."

'I came across those words right after I had left the monastery,' Michael explained reflectively, 'when I'd decided to marry. They touched me deeply and seemed a perfectly apt description of the way I felt. Has that ever happened to you? I hope so. It's such a wonderful feeling.'

Kathy nodded vigorously and was mesmerised by his voice; she too was much taken by the poet's words. During her reading on Christmas night she had encountered such a poem. It had been sonnet twenty-two of Elizabeth Barrett Browning's *Sonnets from the Portuguese*.

'Yes, the other night when I read something by Elizabeth Barrett Browning!'

Eagerly Kathy flipped forward some pages in the anthology until she located the poem she wanted. Handing the volume back to Michael, she pointed: 'Read it!'

Kathy wished, in a way, that it was the late eighteenth or early nineteenth century of Wordsworth's and the Brownings' day, and that she and Michael were gentry living on an English country estate. Every day they would go on long horseback rides through the forest or along the coast of Cornwall, and at night they would return to their home, sit around the fireplace and read to each other. She certainly did not want to think about returning to the hustle and bustle of university life in Orono in a week; being here alone with Michael, with no distractions and with such peace and quiet, was too pleasant. How could she ever want to go back to the more formal student-teacher relationship situations back there warranted for them?

When Michael had finished reading the sonnet, he looked at Kathy with a smile.

'I think,' Kathy continued, 'she described our situation very well. We're here together now. Let's not think about when we must return to school. Let's be happy and make the best of this precious time.'

11

At 10.30 Kathy went upstairs to bathe. Afterward she sat in her room combing her hair trying to decide how to go about seducing a man and succeeding. It hardly seemed like a difficult task!

A short while later she heard that Michael was showering. *Maybe*, Kathy thought, *he was pondering the same question. Surely he would know how to go about it.* And he did, but was still concerned about choosing the right moment. As Michael returned to his room he noticed Kathy was reading in bed. She had left her door wide open.

Cursing himself for a timorous, indecisive fool, Michael went on to his room. *Carpe diem!* Seize the day! kept flitting through his mind. He heard when Kathy crept downstairs a while later. Still he remained lying awake in bed for fifteen or twenty more minutes. Finally he decided to go down to her. Quietly he left his room and paused at the top of the stairs. Kathy sat on the sofa reading by the yellow glow of a lamp; she had stoked up the fire.

'Couldn't you sleep?' Michael asked as he came and sat on the sofa.

Kathy shook her head negatively, smiling, 'I'm sorry I disturbed you.'

'You didn't. I couldn't sleep either,' he admitted. 'What are you reading?'

He could see she was reading in the anthology of English literature he had given her, but wanted to know what poet and what poem.

'William Blake,' Kathy answered.

Michael drew closer to look upon the page Kathy had open and saw she was reading Blake's poem: "The Clod and the Pebble".

'It's one of those special poems we sometimes come across that says exactly what we'd say if we could write verse,' Kathy continued. 'Isn't it a lovely poem? I adore what the clod says.'

Michael smiled in agreement, nodding; Kathy decided now was as good a time as any to bring up what was on her mind.

'We're alone, Michael, absolutely alone, and...' Kathy paused, gathering up her last ounce of courage, 'I'd like us to make love. I sense you share my feelings.'

Michael nodded almost imperceptibly, looking intently into Kathy's eyes. Taking the book from her hands, he laid it aside and then pulled her close to him in a kiss. He would not allow his misgivings about this to interfere any longer.

'There's no one else around but the "baars",' Kathy giggled.

'The "baars" are asleep.'

'Then we are *all* alone.'

'Bullwinkle's not asleep,' Michael teased.

'Well, Bullwinkle can mind his own business. No stopping tonight.'

'No stopping tonight.' Michael kissed her again.

'Let's go upstairs,' Kathy whispered a few minutes later, and they went to Michael's room.

Later on Kathy could clearly recall neither how she nor Michael had undressed. She thought they had removed each others' clothes. In any case, she had not felt the apprehension or embarrassment she had long expected she would feel when disrobing in front of a man. Everything had happened spontaneously. They had acted as a unity in mind, body and spirit – the way making love should be, but too rarely was for most couples. Neither had been anxious or in a hurry; they had no reason to be. The whole cabin smelled of pine needles and flowers due to the incense and potpourri Michael customarily burned. These pleasant aromas, and the poetry and soothing music of the last few days would always be associated in Kathy's and Michael's memories with this special night.

Michael woke first the following morning. The sun was only barely succeeding in peeping through the thick white clouds. Quietly Michael dressed, being careful not to waken Kathy. This morning he had a lot on his mind. He went to the kitchen and lit the stove so that he could have his morning tea. *How did he feel?* Michael could not quite describe his feelings. Last night had indeed been beautiful; he did not regret it exactly. It had not changed his opinion of Kathy, but had, as it should have done, made him love her more. But there was something! *What was it?* Certainly Michael had been completely physically involved in their love making, but his mind and spirit had been detached. His mind and spirit had not been consummately involved! Michael was confused; he could not understand this bizarre reaction. He did not feel he had committed a sin, as he would have felt earlier; he just felt he loved Kathy in a way that went beyond sexuality, though it did not preclude it. Last night he had been mistaken in thinking he *needed* to make love with her. Already he had been with her in heart, mind and soul; their sexual union was merely an outward expression of their love. *Merely? Were his feelings right?* Michael wondered, but did not mean in regard to church rules of right and wrong. He meant, rather, was he being honest and fair with Kathy? *What was he missing?* Michael wondered. *What mistake was he making in having such thoughts? Love*

139

making should be a sacramental act, as holy and as sanctified as consuming the Host during the Eucharist. Now Michael felt he had betrayed Kathy because he had failed to see their love making as the sacrament it was. Michael went back to Kathy. As he joined her in bed once more, she awoke and smiled as she recalled all that had occurred. With a complete passion that he lacked last night, Michael kissed her, and Kathy responded as eagerly as before.

'I think we should get married?' he said later while still holding Kathy close.

Kathy raised up and looked into his face; she had on a large smile.

'When?' she asked.

'Well, I'm not sure. You've got to finish school. When you graduate, I suppose, but you must go on for your master's degree too. I fear we have a rather complicated situation now.'

'Why complicated? Many students are married, especially grad students.'

'They're not married to someone who teaches at their school!'

'You're not my teacher now. You were wise about that. If you were a music teacher, it would be different.' Kathy crawled out of bed and started dressing. 'Let's not worry about all that now. Let's remember our resolution and not think of any of those problems while we're here. This is *our* retreat, and it's no one else's concern what we do here. Of course I shall finish my schooling. It will be nice for us both to be teachers when we marry."

'How would you like to live in England?' Michael asked as he too got out of bed and started getting dressed again.

'I'd love it!' Kathy said excitedly. 'Do you want to go back there?'

'I think so. I miss it. We could live out in the country

and have a garden and some animals. Wouldn't that be nice?'

'Yes! Maybe we could take Candy to England!'

'Of course. You wouldn't mind living so far away from your family?'

'I'd miss them naturally,' Kathy admitted, and sat on the bed and combed her hair, 'but we would visit them now and then. They could come to visit us. You mean you're willing to sell the cabin?'

'I love it here. It's very beautiful, but I do miss England.'

'Could we live in Cornwall?'

'Cornwall? Why are you attracted to Cornwall?'

'I read the *Poldark* series by Winston Graham and, I thought I'd like to live there. You don't like Cornwall?'

'It's fine. It's nearly next door, so to speak, from where I was born. Sure, we could live there. It would depend, on whether I could find a job near enough, whether you could get into a local college, and whether we could find a cottage we liked. I'm sure it would all work out.'

Michael walked over to the window and looked out. The sky was still pale and the clouds thick. He believed it would snow again; he feared it might snow a lot.

'Do you reckon I'd pick up a British accent after I've lived there a while?' Kathy grinned, and joined Michael at the window.

She was in a mischievous, playful mood, which Michael always found delightful.

'You probably will, but I'd bet native Cornishmen would still invariably ask you where you're from,' Michael teased, infected with Kathy's mood. 'Come on. Let's go have some breakfast.'

An hour later light snow began falling; half an hour after that, the snowfall increased, as did the velocity of the wind. Michael gauged the wind was blowing from the northwest, and turned on the radio for a weather report. A snowstorm was forecast, with snowfall accumulations for interior Maine of up to eighteen inches. Already there were fourteen inches on the ground.

'Looks like we're going to be here a while, Kat,' Michael said, calling her 'Kat' for the first time.

'That suits me just fine,' she said with a smile, and contentedly sipped hot chocolate.

Michael checked the woodpiles again. Unless he and Kathy were holed up until July, he was certain they would have enough fuel. The propane gas tank was filled only last week; it should suffice too. Michael even checked the food stocks in the cabinets. Kathy watched him curiously.

'Will you relax?' she said after a few minutes. 'We're going to be fine.'

An hour later, as the snow continued falling, they sat in front of the fireplace. Suddenly Kathy hopped up, having thought of something. Running up to her room, she quickly returned.

'This is a profound little book!' she said and referred to the *Bhagavad Gita* which she had gone to retrieve.

'I'm glad to learn you agree with me.'

'You know, it was funny how you suggested I read this. The very next Monday in Mr Curry's class we started studying *A Passage to India*; Mr Curry gave us a brief but comprehensive overview of Hinduism, Islam and Buddhism, since it helps to know about those religions to fully enjoy the novel, and I had already gotten through almost half of the *Gita* by then. Consequently, it helped me in Mr Curry's class.'

Michael smiled, and noted that Kathy's manner of expression had changed during the last few months.

'What about the *Gita* impresses you?' he asked.

'We'll go into that, but first I'd like to ask how, since

you're a devout Catholic, you can admire a Hindu religious text. Doesn't it contradict or disagree with your church's doctrines?'

'In my interpretation, the *Gita* agrees with the teachings of Jesus, for the most part, anyway. In my study of the world's religions I've discovered they all teach the same truths. Maybe it's a mystical understanding, and, you're right, the Church would probably consider some of my beliefs objectionable. I can live with that because the Church is only a base upon which I build. First of all I listen to the Holy Spirit.'

'But how can you be sure it's the Holy Spirit you're hearing? It might instead be the devil or your own mind.'

'I'm not certain I can explain, except to say the Holy Spirit will never contradict revealed truth nor will it tell me to do something that's wrong.'

'What about last night and this morning? During Thanksgiving break you felt making love with me would be wrong. Now do you feel it was a sin?'

'No, I don't *feel* it was a sin, but I don't know for sure. I'm not going to worry about it, and I don't regret it. Do you?'

'Of course not! I think it was beautiful!'

'Yes, it was.'

'Then why do you seem so sad? You try to hide it, but I see nevertheless.'

'Do I?' He had sincerely not been aware of it.

'You do. You seem lost and full of woe.'

'I'm sorry.'

'Are you sure you don't regret that we came here together?'

'No, Kathy, I don't. I swear I don't. I'm just confused.'

'About what?'

'When we go back to Orono how are we going to act? I don't think it will be quite as it was before we came here.

143

What are we going to do?'

Kathy pondered his question a few minutes.

'We'll just play it cool when we're in public, that's all. We'll be most discreet. This term will be over in a few months. I'll attend summer school too so that I'll graduate even sooner. We can be a little freer in the summer perhaps. It'll work out! Don't worry so much.'

'I'll try,' Michael said, deciding 'Qué sera, sera' would henceforth be his attitude.

Being here now, as Ram Dass, had taught following the Eastern traditions, was the right way to be. Though Michael had known the truth of it for years, it was another matter to keep it always in mind. It had to be lived; it was not merely a sound piece of advice that one could take or leave. Accepting whatever happened as the will of God, or as Karma, was the proper thing to do. It was usually, perhaps invariably, when one tried to shift events around to suit the temporal self that one brought on anger and frustration. This truth had nothing to do with the initiative of trying to make a better life for oneself and one's family, but with accepting adversities and daily, ordinary sorrows as the way of life.

'Were you very involved in the Sixties?' Kathy asked, nudging Michael out of his philosophical reverie.

'Yes, I suppose I was. All that was going on shaped and moulded me. A lot of the images of those times still haunt me, and I like the Sixties rock and folk music better than anything I hear on the radio today. Why?'

'It was a wild time, wasn't it?'

'Yes, but I don't think anything was resolved. All the same social problems exist still, and the economic situation is worse. No one believes in anything today, it seems to me. That type of nihilism exploded into general consciousness then, and though I couldn't see it at the time (I was too young and caught up in everything), I see

144

now that it's made a detrimental impact on our culture. There is a John Lennon song called "God". I think it was released in 1970 or 71. At the time I agreed with it, except for its denial of religious belief, but today I can't accept Lennon's perspective at all. Let me play it for you.'

Michael hopped up and quickly located his old LP copy of John Lennon's *Plastic Ono Band* album and played the song. Kathy listened carefully to the lyrics, especially to the remarks: "God is a concept by which we measure our pain", and the long list of ideas and items in which Lennon no longer believed at the time he wrote the song.

'I can understand Lennon's point of view because I've been there also. I know what it's like when a dream is over. We all have experienced disillusionment at some time or other, but how could he finally decide that all he believed in was himself? That would be depressing,' Michael said seriously.

'He says: "I believe in Yoko and me." He meant he believed in love, don't you think?'

'Yes, and that's good, of course, but I still require more than love between myself and another human being. I hope it doesn't hurt you for me to admit that. I don't mean to diminish our love, but I believe it's only a small intimation of what God will one day show all of us.'

Kathy smiled, 'I know what you mean and I'm not hurt. You're honest, and I believe God must be first in our hearts too. What other songs from the Sixties did you especially like? Was John Lennon one of your favourite performers?'

'Yes, I was much influenced by him and his music. The Beatles were my favourite rock and roll group, and I also admired folk music. Bob Dylan, Donovan and Peter, Paul and Mary also profoundly reached me.'

'You really are a lot like Mr Curry, aren't you?'

Kathy knew Mark was a great fan of those artists also,

145

and taught their lyrics in his classes.

'Oh yeah, we have much in common. We think alike most of the time.'

'Play me some more of the music you like from those days.'

Michael chose Dylan's "Oxford Town", "Blowin' in the Wind", "The Times Are a Changin' " and "Masters of War", and explained them to Kathy. He told her about some of the events which inspired Dylan to write those songs, such as the controversy caused when blacks wanted to enrol in the University of Mississippi in Oxford, and all the other racial tensions of the era; and he explained about the circumstances behind the war in Vietnam, how few people believed in the war, and all the anti-war protests that occurred. Michael gave similar lessons after playing Peter, Paul and Mary's versions of "500 Miles", "Where Have All the Flowers Gone", and "Cruel War". Kathy's first thought was of how depressing such songs were, but that was before the power of the lyrics snared her attention. As she pondered the words and allowed the images Michael's explanations brought into her mind to touch her sensitivities, she began to understand folk music's attraction and importance. It reached into people's souls and summoned up their compassions and senses of outrage over what was unjust. Little or none of those types of message songs were written today. The general attitude, wrought by the 'Me' decade and all the shocks of the past twenty years, had degenerated the majority's attitude to one of 'I don't give a damn.'

As the snowstorm continued during the next four days, Kathy learned more from Michael about the last twenty-five to thirty years than she had learned in history and sociology classes in high school and college. More importantly, she learned how to think. She would never just hear the pounding drums or roaring guitars of pop songs again, but would give the lyrics her keenest attention. In fact, she doubted if she could ever like a song again merely because its tune appealed to her. It would have to say something that touched her heart or mind. And when she mentioned that she liked to watch *Star Trek*, both the old and new shows, Michael took her on another type of educational ride. Being a longtime fan of *Star Trek* also, Michael had the first four major films and a number of the television episodes.

Since they had time to spare, they watched several which Michael chose especially because of their excellence or moral value. The original series episode: 'City on the Edge of Forever', was one of Michael's favourites and he shared it with Kathy; she had never seen it before. After watching *Star Trek: The Motion Picture*, they discussed how V'ger's wish to merge with its creator was akin to mankind's ultimate goal of becoming atoned, at-one-with, God Who is the All. Because of the issues raised in *The Wrath of Khan*, they compared Spock's self-sacrifice with the Christian ethic of giving up one's life for one's friends. Of the *Star Trek* movies Michael favoured *The Voyage Home*. Kathy agreed with his choice; both of them appreciated its ecological messages and its kind regard for other life forms. The episode called 'The Measure of Man' from the *Next Generation* series also elicted an in-depth discussion. The show raised the question of how one can judge sentience; the story dealt with a trial in which an official wanted to disassemble Commander Data, the android, because he felt Data was only a machine. Michael tied it in with the prevalent attitude among people that plants and animals could be disposed of to suit human convenience or greed. Like the American Indians and other so-called primitive peoples, Michael believed reverence and respect were due to all life forms, and the earth and the vast universe were included in that designation. To

147

wantonly kill an animal or a tree was murder in Michael's view. What right did we have to judge those lives were unimportant? Why did people agree they had no right to take a man or woman's life, but every right to kill a deer for sport or a chicken because it scratched up a flowerbed? Kathy, playing Devil's Advocate, pointed out the verse in the book of Genesis: "Let them (humankind) have dominion over the fish of the sea, the birds of the air, and the cattle, and over all the wild animals and all the creatures that crawl on the ground."

"To have dominion over" was an unfortunate way of expressing man's place in the world, Michael thought. It should say "protective custody" he felt. The attitude that he was superior to all other life was typical of man's arrogance, and, Michael ventured to add, it accounted for all the wars, all the pollution and depletion of natural resources, all the rampant destruction and other woes mankind had wrought on the earth and wished to carry out into space also.

'Have you felt this way for long?' Kathy asked, hoping to lighten his mood.

'Yes, but it's been building up inside me more and more during the last ten or twelve years. Maybe it's the letdown that came sometime after I realised all the ideals I once had were never going to come true. Jack Newfield, in his biography of Robert F Kennedy, wrote something I've never forgotten since I first read it. His words touched me profoundly, and not only me, but several generations. Newfield very eloquently expressed something we all felt.' Michael reached over and took a paperback book from the shelf; its title was *Robert F. Kennedy: A Memoir*.

'I want to read this passage to you word for word, for Newfield said it better than I ever could. "Now I realised," Michael read and explained Newfield had written it just after Senator Robert Kennedy had been assassin-

148

ated, "what makes our generation unique, what defines us apart from those who came before the hopeful winter of 1961, and those who came after the murderous spring of 1968. We are the first generation that learned from experience, in our innocent twenties, that things were not really getting better, that we shall not overcome. We felt, by the time we reached thirty, that we had already glimpsed the most compassionate leaders our nation could produce, and they had all been assassinated. And from this time forward, things would get worse: our best political leaders were part of memory now, not hope. The stone was at the bottom of the hill and we were alone." Though I may not precisely be of that particular generation, (I mean I was only fifteen when Robert Kennedy was killed, not in my twenties), I was as deeply affected by those events as Newfield was. Though I was in England, and most of the events happened here in the United States, I was a part of them. Back then America was the coolest place to live, it was believed by the rest of the world. America set the trends and was the world power. We all watched what went on here carefully. People may not realise it today, but all the frustration and disenchantment in our societies stems largely from what happened then. People still had hope. They still believed certain political leaders could help us make a better life for all. People still had faith in their religious institutions and pastors, although our religious alienation had already begun. Now what do we have? The government is a farce. We thought it was a farce then, but now it's even worse! Watergate did it in finally, and the aftermath of the fiasco in Vietnam. I can't name one politician I'd trust to turn my back!'

'What can we do about it?'

'I don't have the answer either, I'm afraid, Kat. I'm probably one of the most confused of all. Maybe the only

149

option is to live as the *Bhagavad Gita* teaches – that is, not to worry and fret over the evil in the world. Like Jesus said: "Give to Caesar what is Caesar's". Maybe we should do the best we can to be happy despite all the rest.'

'You know what I think,' Kathy said, smiling mischievously.

Michael's expression indicated he was eager to hear what she thought.

'I think,' Kathy continued, 'that you *think* too much. Sure we must do the best we can. That's all God could expect, isn't it? And it's God who matters, not society. All the violence, all the murders of people, animals, trees, all the pollution – it's all the *karma* of the perpetrators, isn't it? I'm not suggesting we turn our backs on it and not try to stop all these things, but at the same time we must carry on as joyfully as possible making sure we aren't guilty also.'

Michael kissed her and was proud of her. If there were such things as soul-mates, Kathy was truly his. He would not let social convention take her away from him. As long as she wanted to be with him, he would keep her and strive to be joyful, as she suggested. For now he was content as the snow continued to pile up and the wind blow. He and Kathy had a cosy little nest and a world of ideas, and they had each other and God: what more could they want? When God had provided them with all they needed to survive, what more was it appropriate to desire?

12

Classes resumed on the thirteenth of January, but because of the snowstorm Michael and Kathy were unable to return to Orono. The department of transportation did an excellent job of clearing the roads, and Michael's truck had four-wheel drive; it probably could have got them safely back, but Michael chose not to risk it. Michael's failure to report for his classes was noted immediately, but Kathy was not missed right away except by her closest friends. Her teachers noted she did not answer their rolls, but took no special attention to the fact on the first two days. Donna soon became particularly worried about her friend, and on the second evening after Kathy should have returned, called Kathy's parents. Donna feared Kathy had become sick during the holidays. Neither Kathy nor Michael had told anyone their plans, but the people closest to them suspected their relationship.

On the afternoon of the sixteenth Kathy and Michael got back into town. Michael went to his department chairman's office at once and explained the reason for his late arrival. Doctor Cook was understanding about it, as Michael expected. Kathy had a different reception. Donna was the first to see Kathy as she came lugging her bags back into the dormitory. Kathy was surprised to learn of the uproar she had caused, to learn that her parents were down at the Pine Crest motel awaiting any news the police or university administration could give them. Immediately Kathy called them, and they rushed over with great relief.

Kathy explained that she had gone visiting with a friend and had gotten snowed in. She tried to be casual about it, but her parents, as to be expected, wanted to know all about her friend. *Who was she? It was not true, as some had suspected that Kathy had gone off with Dr Michael Lenard, was it?* A bit shamefacedly Kathy said no; she had been with her boyfriend. Mrs Herrington gasped in horror, and Mr Herrington was more subtly appalled by his daughter's behaviour.

'Kathy! You don't mean you went off with a boy and spent several nights with him, do you?' Kathy's mother asked.

'Yes, Mother. I'm not a child now, you know.'

'Can we meet the young man?' Mr Herrington asked. 'Where is he now?'

'You'll meet him in time. He's not here now.'

From then on Kathy's mother began seeing her daughter differently than she had done before. She treated Kathy more as an adult, although she never condoned her daughter's behaviour. Mr Herrington did not treat Kathy differently at all, but he felt her morals were typical of the younger generation. Morals had been shot to hell twenty-five years ago or more he felt.

The police had nothing to say about it, but they were relieved the young woman was safe; the university officials, though relieved also, had a rumour with which to deal. Had Dr Lenard and the Herrington girl been away together? Could it be only coincidence that they returned the same day after having been missing the same amount of time? It would be of no use to ask either of them point-blank, they felt, but in the next few weeks Michael and Kathy would be more closely watched. There was also a similar potential scandal, they were fully aware, with Mr

Hoffman and one of the nursing students.

Mark told Michael of all the rumours that had been going around during the last three days, and Michael judged he and Kathy would have to be even more discreet than they already expected. Though he wondered who started the rumour, Michael decided it was one of those things he would not worry about. It was not that he did not see the complications it might cause, but rather that he was assured of his and Kathy's love for one another, and firmly believed it was no one's business.

The presence of Kathy's parents made her life more complex than usual. There was always a tenseness and uneasiness in the air whenever they were together now. Kathy did her best to act normally, like her usual self, but it was difficult. Her mother was anguished; her baby was no longer her baby (Kathy's rank as third of four children had no bearing on Mrs Herrington's attitude; all her children were her babies and would remain so if she should live to see then when they were 50 years old), and Mrs Herrington could not accept it. The woman knew she had to accept it, since she had no choice, but it was going to be one of the hardest tasks she ever had to do.

'What is your boyfriend's name, dear?' Mrs Herrington asked as she, Mr Herrington and Kathy were having dinner at Bangor's Sequino's Italian Restaurant on the evening of the sixteenth.

Kathy had by now concluded that honesty was the best policy, and admitted his name was Michael.

'Isn't that the given name of that teacher some people are insinuating you were with?' Mr Herrington said between mouthfuls of his *Bacella Napolitano*.

'Yes,' Kathy admitted, her eyes downcast, 'I know I first told you he wasn't my boyfriend, but in fact he is. Doctor Michael Lenard and I were together during the last week, but you must not tell anyone. Please, Mama,

Daddy! He could lose his job, you understand.'

Still reeling from this latest shock, Mr Herrington had to be told by his wife to keep his voice down. 'Maybe he should lose his job! What right does he have to carry on with young girls? It's criminal! Damn right, I'm going to tell on the bastard!'

'No, Daddy! We're going to be married! I love Michael and he loves me. Why doesn't he have the right to see whoever he chooses? I'm *not* a little girl! I'm twenty years old, and . . . you make it seem like he took me off by force!'

'Can we meet him?' The mother wondered again, wishing to avoid causing more attention in the restaurant and to prevent an argument developing further.

'Yes, mama, of course. I think you should.'

'Are you through?' Mr Herrington said as he rose from his chair. 'Let's go meet the son of a bitch now.'

Although Kathy was not finished with her meal (she had hardly eaten anything), she was glad to leave the restaurant. As they got into the rented car she said, 'I think I should arrange a meeting. I wouldn't want to just burst in on him unannounced.'

'Why the hell not? If you're going to marry him, it shouldn't matter if you dropped in. Where does he live?'

It was clear her father was bound and determined to meet Michael this evening, to engage him in a fist-fight perhaps, and though Kathy felt uneasy about it, she agreed. Fifteen minutes later they were knocking at Michael's door. Fortunately Michael was home.

'Kathy!' Michael exclaimed as he opened the door, and it was clear he was glad to see her. The Herrington's scrutinised him from head to toe, both of them trying to decide if they liked his looks or not. Mrs Herrington was surprised to see a young man; she had expected an older one for some reason. Rather a nice looking fellow, she thought.

'Please come in,' Michael said as invitingly as he could manage. 'Sit down. Can I offer you something?' He was sure to dispense with all the friendly gestures, hoping to make a good impression.

'This is my father, Carl Herrington, and my mother Evelyn. They flew up here because Donna called them when I wasn't back. Michael is from England.'

'Yes, I recall you mentioning that in one of your letters,' Mrs Herrington remarked as she sat down, making sure the couch was clean beforehand. Subtly, but thoroughly, she began to examine the entire room.

'So, you want to marry my daughter, do you?' the father asked, plopping down on the sofa as though it were his own in front of the television set at home. Kathy sat between her parents and Michael took the chair nearby.

'Yes, sir. Kathy and I have decided we would like to get married. We think we'll wait until she graduates.' Michael hoped that latter statement would appease them somewhat.

'Have you ever been married before?' Evelyn Herrington wondered, having noticed a photograph of a young woman hanging on the wall.

'Yes, ma'am, but my wife died. That's Angela in the picture.' Michael saw where the woman's eyes had just rested.

'You don't have any children?'

'No sir. We were married only a year prior to her death.'

'Michael was . . . ' Kathy almost said Michael was a monk before his marriage, but suddenly realised it would be best to avoid the topic of religion as long as possible.

'Yes, Kathy, what were you about to say?' Mr Herrington asked.

'I was going to explain that Michael is a philosopher and he's written essays and articles which have been

155

published.'

'Are you sure I can't offer you something?' Michael wondered again, feeling very uncomfortable.

'What part of England are you from?'Mrs Herrington asked, trying to sound genuinely interested, but refusing his offer of refreshments.

'Lyme Regis, ma'am. It's a small town on the south western coast. My father was a fisherman and my mother a housewife. I haven't any brothers or sisters, though I always wished I had one or two.'

'How old are you, sir?' Mr Herrington demanded in his imperious manner.

'I am thirty-nine.'

'Don't you think you're too old for my daughter?'

'I was concerned about the age discrepancy between Kathy and myself until she assured me it made no difference to her.'

'Carl, remember that you are eleven years older than me,' Evelyn remarked, trying to be fair despite herself.

Giving his wife a reproving glare, Carl said. 'Well, I know, Evelyn, but, my God, Kathy's only twenty years old!'

'I was eighteen when you married me!'

Kathy and Michael looked at each other and grinned as they listened to her parents' interchanges.

'Did you say you have a Ph.D.?' Carl asked as he turned his attention back to Michael.

'Yes, sir,' Michael responded, trying to recall when he mentioned it. *He hadn't, had he?*

'Michael went to Cambridge University, Dad.'

'Cambridge! Damn fine school that! Why'd you come to the United States?'

'I came here shortly after my wife died. I'd been teaching at a college in London, but I was tired of the scene. I needed to get away from all the sights that

156

reminded me of Angela.'

'What was wrong with your wife?' Evelyn asked, immediately wishing she had rephrased her question.

'She had cancer, Mrs Herrington. She was only thirty-four years old.'

'How long has it been?'

'It's been six years.'

'So, you and Kathy want to marry, and you think you'll wait until she finishes school, that right?' Carl said, changing the subject; he could not handle sentimentality.

'I don't know, sir.' Michael looked to Kathy. 'I mean we're sure we want to marry, but we haven't decided when yet. I think it would be best if we waited until she finishes school. I want to do what's best for her.'

'I'm glad to hear it, yet you thought it was all right for the two of you to go away to a cabin in the woods during a snowstorm.'

'Daddy, when we left there was no snowstorm!'

'That aside then,' Carl continued irately, 'you thought it was okay to take her off like that without telling a soul.'

Michael wanted to hold his ground, and was careful to maintain his composure. 'We didn't feel it was anyone's business. Who do you think we should've told? If you and Mrs Herrington decided one weekend to make a trip to Savannah or Florida, would you call and tell us about it? Why should you?'

'That would be different. We're married and older than Kathy.'

'Do you feel Kathy is immature for her age? Do you not think she's an intelligent, responsible young lady? Don't you trust her, sir?'

'I did until she pulled this stunt,' the man said gruffly, glaring at his daughter.

Kathy stood up and started pacing through the room, 'I'm sorry you feel as you do, Daddy. I'd hoped you'd

157

understand a little better. I'm not quite sure just what it is you and Mama find so objectionable, but that's really beside the point. I *am* an adult now, and you both must face that fact. I've done nothing I'm ashamed of, and I do not want to be estranged from either of you. The fact is that I love Michael, and he loves me, and I've no doubt that one day we shall be married. Can't you just accept that and let us all live peacefully together?'

After her spiel Kathy sat down on the footstool in front of Michael's chair. After several minutes of tense silence and cautious glances, Mr Herrington rose and his wife followed suit.

'All right, Kathy, like you said, you're an adult now. Do whatever the hell you like. We won't stop you.' Though Carl's manner remained gruff, Kathy was sure he would come around in time. At least several important issues had been addressed, and Kathy's spirit felt freer than before. 'Come on, let's go. All I can say is that this is a hell of a note!' Carl added.

'No, Mama, you and Daddy go on. I'll see you later.'

'It was good that we met tonight,' Michael said and reached out his hand to shake the parents' hands. Evelyn responded kindly; Carl gave Michael's hand only the barest and briefest grasp.

'You'll come by the motel before going to your room, won't you?' Evelyn asked and Kathy nodded.

After she had heard her parents drive away, Kathy turned to Michael and sighed, 'Well, what do you think?'

'It'll work out, I think. Their reaction was normal, I guess, though they really have had a hold on you. Your breaking free had to happen eventually. Now, hopefully, you will build a new relationship with them, one that will be maturer and respectful on both sides. Are you all right?'

Kathy looked worn out from the ordeal, but she assured

158

Michael she was fine. He pulled her to him in an embrace, hoping to give her consolation. 'Try to get a good night's rest after you see them. Let's remember our advice to each other about not worrying.'

Michael walked her nearly to the motel and she gave him a sweet kiss before they said goodnight. Her parents were still discussing the situation when Kathy arrived.

'Well, what do you think of Michael?' she asked as she sat down at the dresser.

'He seems to be a nice fellow,' Evelyn said and offered a small smile.

'He is, Mama. Michael is very nice and kind. When you know him better I'm sure you'll agree.'

'I suppose you've slept with him by now,' Carl asked, never one to respect anyone's privacy. In his family he tried to maintain the authority of an ancient Roman *paterfamilias*.

'Carl!' Evelyn cautioned.

Kathy did not answer.

'Yeah, and what happens if he gets you pregnant? What then, if you haven't finished school?' Carl went on to ask, his face red from his elevated blood pressure.

'I won't get pregnant until I'm ready,' Kathy insisted.

Carl laughed, 'Oh sure, that's what you young girls always think!'

Kathy saw no point in pursuing the matter. 'When is your flight back to Atlanta, Mama?'

'We don't leave until Sunday afternoon.'

'No doubt we're in your way,' Carl said sarcastically.

'Of course not. I'm glad you'll be here several days more. We'll have most of the weekend, and hopefully you will come to like Michael better.'

The very next day the first thing Mr Herrington did was go to Dean Sike's office. He had mulled over the situation during the night and had decided he just could not accept it. The dean was about to leave for lunch when his secretary told him Herrington wanted to speak with him. Reluctantly Sikes agreed to see the man. He had been dreading such a confrontation, and he had also been looking forward to lobster for lunch and it irritated him that his meal would be delayed. Putting on his best front, Sikes invited Kathy's father into the office, and offered him a seat.

Mr Herrington was too angry to sit down, and immediately started telling the dean what he thought of a school that allowed such outrageous behaviour to take place right under its nose and do nothing to stop it.

'Now hold on, Mr Herrington, we don't *allow* intimate relationships between our faculty members and our students, but it's most difficult, as I'm sure you can understand, to monitor all that goes on here. The university is a large organisation, sir, and .... Well, anyway, I'm as upset by the situation between Dr Lenard and your daughter as you are.'

'Why'd you hire the bastard in the first place? Don't you check up on potential employees beforehand? How could this happen? My daughter's only twenty years old!'

'Yes sir, we investigate all faculty applicants thoroughly before we elect to hire anyone. Dr Lenard has an excellent record, not only academically, but he was a monk, for Christ's sake! That fact ought to say enough about his morals, don't you think?'

'A monk! What the hell do you mean? A Roman Catholic monk?'

'Yes, that's right! He had left the monastery to marry, but his wife died not long after they were married. There was nothing scandalous in his background.'

'Well, that just figures! All those Roman Catholic priests are lechers. It's become more and more obvious lately. There was that damned archbishop in Atlanta not long ago. He'd been carrying on an affair with a woman for years. They're all the same!'

'Sir, as far as we know, Dr Lenard has led a very quiet life since he came here about three years ago. He's been a recluse for the most part. I think your daughter must be a special young lady.'

'She is! That's what surprises the hell out of me. How could she do something like this? It must be Lenard's fault. He seduced her, I reckon. He took advantage of her innocence of such matters.'

'Mr Herrington, I don't know how it happened, but I assure you any necessary steps against Lenard will be taken. It hurts the university for such things to occur, and I certainly cannot allow him to get away with any wrongdoings. I'll speak with him, you can count on it.'

Feeling better now, Herrington thanked Sikes and said he would keep in touch. Immediately after leaving the dean's office, Mr Herrington met his wife at a restaurant for lunch and told her what he had learned. She became distraught and could not finish her meal. They decided that later that day they would have another meeting with Kathy and her boyfriend, and this time they would get everything straightened out once and for all. There was no way Evelyn Herrington was going to see her little girl married to a Papist!

The girls in Kathy's dormitory were eager to hear all about her romance, as most girls of their ages would be, and they had been asking her lots of questions ever since her return from the Christmas break. Kathy decided this was not the type of popularity she had ever coveted, and all she wanted now was for things to be back to normal. When Kathy's last class of the day ended, she hurried to the privacy of her room, but found her parents waiting for her in the lounge.

Back at the Herringtons' motel room, the parents

confronted their daughter about Michael's religious background.

'You never told us he was a Roman Catholic, that he had been a monk!' Evelyn said with a pained expression.

'I was going to tell you, but knowing how you'd react, I dreaded it.'

'You can't seriously be considering marrying a Catholic, dear, surely!'

'Mama, you don't understand Michael's religion. All those stories you've heard all your life about Catholics aren't true. I know. I've been going to his church, and they don't worship the Virgin Mary, the Pope or statues. They worship Jesus, just like other Christians.'

'You've been going to his church!' Evelyn seemed more shocked by this revelation than she had been when she learned her daughter was no longer a virgin.

'Yes, not all the time, but enough to understand what they believe, and Michael has taught me much more. I've read books too, and I've learned more about the true meaning of Christianity in these ways than I learned all those years I attended Sunday school at our church.'

Evelyn sat down hard and looked at Kathy dumbfoundedly. 'You can't mean what you're saying. He's poisoned your mind.'

'Mother, really! Why don't you and Daddy come to Mass with me this coming Saturday night and see for yourselves?'

'We couldn't do that!' Herrington said. 'They wouldn't allow us in the door.'

'Of course they would! They'd be glad to have you. Please come. I think you'd realise the Catholic church isn't like you think it is. Michael's the deacon.'

Glances of uncertainty passed between Kathy's parents. *Would it be an unpardonable sin to attend a Papist service* they wondered. Out of love for their daughter and

162

curiosity, they agreed to think about it at least. Kathy was pleased that she had accomplished that much, and started planning how her parents and Michael could spend more time with one another during the next two days. She decided to go to Michael's apartment later and work out something.

On Friday evening the Herringtons and Kathy and Michael had supper together at Bangor's Greenhouse Restaurant, one of the nicest places in town, and Michael paid for it all. Later they went to a performance by the Bangor Masque Theatre, and it did much to lighten everyone's mood. When Michael said goodbye to the Herringtons that evening he knew he had made progress because Carl gave him a strong handshake and even called him by his first name.

After Mass on Saturday night, once it was explained to Evelyn that Catholics did indeed consider Sunday the Sabbath, Evelyn had to admit the service had moved her, that she had been under certain misconceptions about Catholics. To be honest, she had quite enjoyed the Mass, and had thought the priest's sermon well-written and deeply moving. It was nearly as good, she said, as Brother Harden's sermons were at Calvary Baptist Church back home, if a great deal more subdued. The priest at St Luke's did not put as much emotion into his delivery as did Brother Harden, she added. When she saw her parents' flight off Sunday morning, Kathy felt some of the tension she had felt during the last few days being lifted away with the plane.

The next morning after a faculty meeting, the dean asked Michael to go with him to his office. Michael was prepared for whatever came, and he went with the same attitude he had always had with Dean Sikes.

'Michael, I guess you suspect why I've called you in here. The reason has to do with the rumours that are

going around the campus regarding you and the Herrington girl. Now I don't like to think the worst of my
colleagues, but I cannot allow such gossip to go un-
checked. Why, the girl's parents even flew up here all the
way from Atlanta, Georgia! Tell me and I'll believe you.
Is it true that you are carrying on an affair with the girl?'

Michael remained quiet far longer than he knew he
should, but it was a serious question. If the truth had
already been largely established, he reasoned, he would
cause more trouble by denying it. It would be almost like
admitting he was guilty of something. *What about Kathy's
reputation?* 'I'm in love with her,' he answered finally. 'We
intend to get married.'

Dean Sikes leaned back in his leather chair and looked
at Michael sternly. 'It's true then. There is, shall we just
say, a relationship between you and this student.'

'Yes,' Michael admitted, sighing heavily, 'But Kathy
isn't my student. Neither is she a child. Why do you ask?'

'Well,' Jack Sikes said, reminding Michael of Ronald
Reagan, 'there are these rumours as you probably know.
There's gossip. We can't have them! Such talk makes the
whole university look bad.'

'Why? I don't understand why. The other students
don't care, and most of the faculty aren't interested. They
all have more important matters with which to concern
themselves. No one cares except for certain nosey people
who haven't anything more enlightening to think about.
You're exaggerating and making the university seem like
a small town.'

'Well, it is like a small town, but it also includes a large
community. Parents won't send their sons and daughters
here if they fear the kids will become involved with their
teachers. The girl's father came in here raving mad last
week demanding to know why I allow such things to go
on! Maybe things are different in England, but here

164

student-teacher relationships are strictly impersonal.'

'Really? If Kathy were in one of my classes now I might be able to see your point a little clearer. She need not ever take another course in my department.'

'The girl made an A in your comparative religions class last semester,' Jack said as though making a scoring shot, and proceeded to examine his fingernails.

'She deserved an A. You can examine her work and determine it for yourself. Kathy's made A's in all of her classes because she's intelligent and a diligent student.'

'About two weeks ago the two of you were together at your cabin, isn't that true? You went there after the girl returned from her Christmas visit home.'

'That's none of your business.' Michael was as polite as he could manage.

'Doctor Lenard,' Sikes continued, his manner having become reprimanding and authoritative, 'I'm afraid behaviour like this cannot go on. You must stop seeing the girl, and hopefully all this scandal will die down.'

'I refuse, sir. We love each other, and this is no one's concern but ours.' Michael felt like he had said or thought that for over a month now; he was sick of having to repeat it to everyone.

'Doctor Lenard, I urge you to think this out carefully.'

'Are you threatening to fire me?'

'I hope I won't have to go that far.' Sikes got up and went to stare out the window, turning his back to Michael.

Michael thought for a few minutes and then stood up. 'You won't. I resign.'

Sikes whirled around in stunned disbelief. He had been sure his warning would be sufficient. Though he had known it was possible Michael would resign, Sikes had put the notion aside as most unlikely. Good teaching positions were too hard to come by these days. 'Please

Michael, don't act hastily. You're one of our finest teachers. We'd hate to lose you.'

'You have already done so. Good day to you.'Michael harboured no regrets as he walked out. Resigning was the only right course of action he saw. Glancing at his watch, he saw it was 2.30; Kathy was probably in her voice lesson. Michael went to the old cemetery to think, stopping at the drink machine on his way to buy a Dr Pepper.

Dean Sikes immediately called Dr Cook and told him of what had happened. Monty Cook was angered that it had come to this; Michael was also one of Monty's good friends. The dean wondered if someone could take on Michael's classes, and Monty said he was not sure. He did not say so, but he wanted to speak with Michael and try to persuade him to reconsider. As soon as Dean Sikes hung up, Monty went to Michael's office, but Michael was not there.

For an hour Michael sat on a bench under a venerable oak in deep thought. It was cold, but he only barely noticed. Everything had happened so quickly it was unbelievable. To himself Michael admitted that he had acted impulsively, and recalled how in the past when he acted without due consideration he often regretted it later. As dusk settled around him Michael headed for home. He guessed he would return to his office tomorrow to pack up his books and papers.

While Michael was preparing his supper Dr Cook knocked on the front door. Michael was hoping it was Kathy as he went to open the door for his visitor.

'Hello Monty, I can't say I'm surprised to see you. Come on in.'

'Michael, Jack called me right after you resigned. I went to your office several times but couldn't find you. You can't leave like this. What will we do in the department without you?' Monty was trying to appeal to

Michael's senses of loyalty and duty.

'I apologise for the inconvenience, Monty, but I had no choice. The dean or the president or anyone else has no right to tell me how to live my private life. I was just about to have supper. You want something?'

'No, thank you. My wife will be expecting me later.' Monty followed Michael into the kitchen and sat down at the table while Michael continued preparing his meal. 'I agree with you,' Monty continued, 'but surely something can be worked out. I could insist to Jack that we cannot possibly make do without you, at least this semester. It would make it difficult for us in fact. Stay this semester please, and during the summer you can decide what you want to do.'

'I know what I want to do, Monty. I want to marry Kathy and return to England. We've already been making plans.'

'Yes, good, but you aren't going to marry right away, are you? You had intended to work on until June, hadn't you?'

'Yes, of course, but Sikes isn't going to tell me who I can see and who I can't see. I won't work here under those conditions.'

'I understand, but please, let me talk with him before you take off. As soon as the gossip dies down, and it won't go on much longer, Jack will not be as worried. Do me this favour. Let me convince him that it's imperative that you stay on through this semester.'

Because of Monty's friendship, Michael agreed to wait at least until he heard the outcome of Monty's talk with Sikes. Monty said he would speak with the dean first thing the next morning.

Sikes was pacing the floor Tuesday morning, considering that now he must also deal with the Hoffman situation, and there was also that matter with the sociology professor. It had become a larger matter than he had foreseen. It would indeed be terrible if Hoffman also resigned. Rudy was one of the school's showpieces, being also the conductor of the city orchestra. Sikes was glad to see Monty.

'Jack, I've spoken with Michael. I've tried to persuade him not to go. Our department is short on teachers, as you know. Mrs Andrews is still on maternity leave; she's had some medical complications, and we've never hired anyone since Dr Leissner's death last winter. It would put us in a pinch were Michael to leave right now. If he would only stay until the semester's over, it'd mean a lot to us.'

'I can't put up with the vulgar talk about him and that girl! Surely you can understand. He all but admitted the stories were true. It's scandalous!'

'Jack, the gossip will be gone soon. Such things always fade away. No one really cares anyway, not these days. It goes on more frequently than perhaps you are aware.'

'Oh, I'm aware, believe me! I know about certain other misbehaving members of our esteemed faculty, whom I shall not name. I haven't yet decided how to deal with them.'

'But about Michael ... '

'Do you honestly need him so much? You couldn't possibly have one of your staff take over his classes?'

'No, we're all loaded down as it is, and Michael's the expert in those topics too.'

'Do you think, then, that you could persuade him to stay on until the end of the term?'

'Possibly. I think so.' Monty made a point of sounding uncertain. 'He might do it as a favour to me. He knows how rough we'd have it in his absence.'

'All right, but assure him that I do not condone his behaviour, and that he'd better watch his steps.'

As Monty expected, Michael agreed to remain at his

post as a favour, but he would not stop seeing Kathy. Two weeks later no one whispered or gossiped about the "scandalous" couple any longer. Their attention had become charged by the basketball team's winning streak.

Michael and Kathy saw each other frequently, almost every evening, and they continued making their plans. Kathy felt good about everything now. She was sure it would all work out. In April she registered for summer school, foregoing the promise of carefree warm days of leisure; she wanted to earn her bachelor's degree as soon as possible. (The way she figured it, she would only have to go one more semester after the summer term to complete the requirements.) Michael planned to go to England during June and July to start lining up a job and finding a house with a sizable tract of land. He also intended to devote himself more to his writing; for over three years he had been working on a novel.

After they married and were in England, Kathy would enroll in a university near their home to work on her master's degree. If need be, she would get a part-time job, though Michael doubted that would be necessary. Ever since meeting Kathy, and especially since they had real-ised they loved each other, Michael had felt himself coming back to life. "Though much is taken, much abides," he recalled from Tennyson's *Ulysses*. Now Michael had someone with whom to share his life, and it made everything appear brighter. He would witness Kathy's further maturations, her changes, and see her make new discoveries as he had long wished he could be around to see. After such a long time Michael again felt consummately happy, and he did not fear his joy would be snatched away. Kathy was also completely happy; she had no regrets about all that had happened, and no worries about the future awaiting her. It had been her dream once, one she thought would never come true, to

169

live in the West Country of Devon or Cornwall, and now she would. She even walked straighter with greater self-assurance, and she was no longer bothered by peer pressure. Though she still treasured her friends Donna and Leisa, most of the other girls in the Village, and especially the Sorority sisters, seemed altogether adolescent to her now. Kathy did not avoid them or treat them crassly, but she no longer wanted to be like them or a part of their crowd. They sensed this and were respectful towards her. Everyone could see that Kathy Herrington, the formerly shy, quiet, Georgia Belle had, during the past school year, become a refined lady with a unique style they all envied and tried to emulate.